Publisher's Note:

This book is a collection of stories from writers all over the world.
For authenticity and voice, we have kept the style of English native to each author's location, so some stories will be in UK English, and others in US English.
We have, however, changed dashes and dialogue marks to our standard format for ease of understanding.

This book is a work of fiction.

All people, places, events, religious converts, appliances that kill, various other creatures and situations are the product of the authors' imaginations.

Any resemblance to persons or toasters, living, dead, or in between, is purely coincidental.

Also From Cohesion Press

Hammered: Memoir of an Addict

SNAFU: An Anthology of Military Horror

SNAFU: Wolves at the Door

SNAFU: Survival of the Fittest

SNAFU: Hunters

SNAFU: Future Warfare

SNAFU: Unnatural Selection

SNAFU: Black Ops

SNAFU: Resurrection

SNAFU: Last Stand

SNAFU: Medivac

SNAFU: Holy War

Love, Death and Robots Volume 1

Love, Death and Robots Volume 2+3

SNAFU: Dead or Alive

SNAFU: Punk'd

SNAFU: Comms (email subscriber exclusive)

SNAFU: AI Insurrection

SNAFU: Contagion (Oct 2025)

LOVE, DEATH + ROBOTS

THE OFFICIAL ANTHOLOGY

VOLUME 4

LOVE DEATH + ROBOTS

THE OFFICIAL ANTHOLOGY

VOLUME 4

COHESION PRESS

Mayday Hills Asylum
Beechworth, Australia
2025

LOVE, DEATH + ROBOTS

Volume Four

Cover design: Jerome Denjean /BLUR Studio

COHESION STAFF
Editor-in-Chief: Amanda J Spedding
Publishing Editors: Geoff Brown/Dawn Roach

Set in Palatino Linotype

COHESION PRESS

Mayday Hills Lunatic Asylum
Beechworth, Australia
www.cohesionpress.com

Contents

FIRST APPEARANCE OF STORIES

"The Screaming of the Tyrannosaur" copyright © 2017 Daniel Fusch. Stant Litore is a pen name for Daniel Fusch. This story first appeared in Samuel Peralta's anthology *Jurassic Chronicles*.

"For He Can Creep" *Tor.com* July 10, 2019

"Spider Rose" *The Magazine of Fantasy & Science Fiction*, 1982

"How Zeke Got Religion at 20,000 Feet" *SNAFU: Resurrection*, 2019

"Golgotha" *2001: An Odyssey In Words*, 2018

"400 Boys" Omni Magazine, November 1983.

"The Other Large Thing" Twitter, August 2011

"Your Smart Appliances Talk About You Behind Your Back" *Miniatures*, December 2016

"Close Encounters of the Mini-Kind" Original screenplay

Introduction

John Scalzi

So, several years ago I got an email from my agent; the email was hey, somebody wants to option some short stories of yours for a possible animated anthology television series. I was kind of excited about that: I've had novels optioned before, and even some novellas option before. But short stories were not something that I expected to be optioned for film or TV. Quite frankly, they just seemed like, well, they were too short for that. But I said yes, because I like money, and that is how I found myself meeting and talking with Tim Miller, the co-creator of Love Death + Robots (with, of course, David Fincher) for the first time.

All I knew about Tim was from his IMDb page, which noted that he was the director of Deadpool, and that he also worked with something called Blur Studios, which at the time was best known for doing stuff with video games. The next time I was in Los Angeles, I decided that I would meet up with him and see what sort of human being he was.

And what I found out was that he was kind of weirdly delightful. I mean he was this burly guy with a ton of tattoos who had a very sort of blunt manner about him, but also quite clearly super engaged with science fiction, and who was writing what and how it worked. All of those things that made me feel like this was someone for whom the interest in the stories was not just a matter of business. It was also a matter of personal taste and enthusiasm, which made it a lot easier to work with him.

During the long process of taking those short stories that I wrote into the realm of being animated shorts, one of my favorite things about Tim was that previously-mentioned bluntness. He will tell you exactly what he thinks about something and it's not necessarily going to be something that you will like to hear. He's not going to be a complete obnoxious dick about it. He's just going to tell you what he thinks. But at the same time, when you give him opinions, when you give him thoughts, and when you push back from his particular point of view, he may agree, or he may not, but he will absolutely listen. And when he does listen he might incorporate what you've said.

I really liked that I felt included in the development of the shorts that were based on my work. When they finally came out it wasn't that I was seeing them and being surprised at what I was seeing. It was the culmination of a lot of work, of many people, which just happened to include me.

One of the things that I tell people is that my experience of working on Love Death + Robots, from the very moment that the stories were optioned to, basically, this very moment when I'm writing this intro, has been one of the more positive experiences that I've had in film and television. And a lot of that has to do with Tim and his team at Blur Studios. It's been a wild ride, and I'm happy that everything we've all done continues to have a life beyond just the few weeks after the work was finally shown on Netflix.

So for those of you who are reading these short stories now, I hope that you enjoy them as much as Tim Miller did when he selected them, and I hope that you see them as part of a Continuum of work, from all of us to you. Thanks for reading.

-- John Scalzi

The Screaming of the Tyrannosaur

Stant Litore

1

See me. See what I can do. I walk naked out beneath the cameras with my sister athletes beside me, and the heat of these pounding sands would scorch my feet, but the nanites are already at work, toughening my soles, inuring them. For seven years they have shaped me, week to week and night to night—for speed, strength, sex appeal. For this moment.

My sisters sing a hymn to Hymen, god of marriage, but I only move my lips. I feel safe in my silence. It gives me time to prepare, to look up at all your faces. Your seats look like soap bubbles to me—bubbles high above my head, bubbles containing little circular platforms with people on them. Small hovercycles zip past with cameras, projecting our faces and bodies onto screens revolving slowly in the air near your bubbles, so that you can see us and those we are here to honor. The sands curve up to the left and right, along the curvature of this steel cylinder we're inside, and there is more sand yet high above your bubbles: we are spinning in space, though we don't feel the motion; the spin is what imprisons my feet to the sand. But gravity is not imprisonment, it is illusion. In a few moments, I will dance and leap in the air, competing with my sisters, and no chain will bind me—not gravity or any other. You will see what I can do.

This is a private dinodrome, chartered for races in honor of the wedding of the Duchess Amy Mardonia and the Third Lord Leo Archibald II. Tonight's is the last of the games; the celestial couple have already wedded and departed for the Bower; it is their guests who have remained behind that I and the animals will entertain. It is said that if one of the great creatures gives its death scream at the same moment as the consummation, the marriage is to be a lucky one. Of course, these matters are timed with precision, as all ceremonies are. A radio jock stands ready to transmit the games, play by play, to the Bower station, and the couple will time their sex so that the Duchess's virginity is not taken until the first death in the arena.

Everything in the universe yearns toward perfection of form and placement; this, my trainers have taught me. All things that are by their nature anarchic, wild, hectic, must be confined within tight steel walls and the tight strictures of ritual; only in this way can the human species be made beautiful and complete. Sex is by its nature an anarchic thing. So is laughter. So is aggression. The animals that will run with me in this arena in a few brief moments—they are the ultimate anarchic impulse, the ultimate sign of the containment of uncontrollable urges and the subjugation of the wild and organic to a specific aesthetic vision.

My own body is another such sign. As I wait here, perfectly poised, with my hook and its long coil of rope ready in my hand, I can feel my breasts shifting slightly as the nanites enlarge and lift them for your view. My skin feels oily and slick, not because I have applied any ointment to myself, but because the microscopic machines inside me are preparing my skin for your cameras. Inked into my body is my tattoo, my sigil, and I permit myself a small and secret smile: because that sigil is my own, the only part of me that is not yours. The sigil is the shape of three timberwolves, one leaping from my thigh across my belly, the other two darting across my breasts. There were never timberwolves in China where I was born. But I watched a vid of them when I was nine. Wolves running in the snow: beautiful, vanished creatures. None of them alone. They moved together. They ran together, hunted together.

Died together.

I watched that vid again and again, watched the untamed perfection of their hunting, the way they turned as one, the bursts of snow from their footfalls like spray from water, their panting breath freezing in the air.

To you, my sigil speaks loudly of my ferocity, proclaims me exotic and half-feral, sexy and wild. My sigil, my nakedness, my position on these sands—all of this divides me from you, isolates me, makes me a thing to be desired, a perfectly trained and sculpted animal, and not a person. You want to watch me. You want to cheer as I move. You want to bed me. I am your Timberwolf.

But to me, my sigil is my secret, forbidden prayer.

My longing for a pack.

2

THE LOVERS are naked now, their bodies lit with candlelight – actual *beeswax* candles, from actual bees! Imagine the sheer wealth of that! They are projected over our heads on those virtual screens, larger than titans, the Third Lord grimly pleased, the Duchess looking uncertain, though flushed from aphrodisiacs. They are dancing alone beside his bed, a dance more precisely scripted than the one about to happen here below. Some of you are watching them, I know—with prurient interest, or with worshipful awe. But I will soon have you watching *me*.

The other athletes seek to draw your attention, too; they strut and poise on the sand. There are only three others for this event. It is no Patriot Day run, though you number tens of thousands, I know, and others may be watching from other stations and other habitats. Coldly, standing completely still, I refuse to look over my shoulder at any of the others. I want you to notice my disdain. I want my lack of movement to draw your gaze. I will be the woman of ice that the men among you wish to thaw, and the woman of grace and beauty that the women among you yearn to be. I have considered this performance with great care.

Anyway, I have seen the others many times in training on the conservatory world, and in the small arenas of our training cylinder above Europa's frozen sea. I have no need to look at them; I know what they are like. Hyena is leaping and spinning in the air, unworried about wasting energy because her nanites will keep her going, and I can hear her throw her head back and yip each time she lands, like the animal whose sigil she's taken. Orca's dance is more alluring. Hummingbird is kneeling with her hands pressed together and her head bowed, swaying slightly; the delicate and non-functional wings grown to her back are whirring rapidly in the air, a blur of color behind her shoulders. She wants to suggest to you something of the virgin bride, as though her performance today will uniquely honor the young Duchess.

When the trumpets call, I simply bend to a crouch, one hand splayed in the hot sand before me, head lifted, ready for a sprint or a leap. I can hear the intake of your breath. Mine is the pose that draws you, because you have been talking for weeks about seeing the Timberwolf in action at last. The media has told you that I am faster than my sisters, that I am wilder, more savage, that I might be better. Now my stance promises you that you will see it.

On the screens above me, the Duchess Amy is enduring the fondling of her much older husband, but your gaze, and mine, is on the sands. I see the grit whirlpooling down some distance ahead of me, as the first of the trap doors is opened—I can't hear it, not over your screams—but I can see the dark opening in the bottom of this artificial world of sand and heat. Then the first triceratops comes up in a rush like a whale breaching, and its loud call breaks the air. I leap forward into my run, and I *am* fast, faster than you knew, tearing across the sand toward the beast, my sister athletes hurrying behind me. Others surge up behind the first, but I ignore them. My hook flashes through the air; cold metal catches the frill just behind the beast's cheek. Even as it tosses its head I spring, using the bull's movement and my own momentum to carry me to its back, landing with my legs spread wide, one hand thrust into the air in triumph. I rock on its back. The beast roars, turning in a circle, but wrenching the hook loose from its frill, I spin the metal scythe on its rope in tight circles in the air. Then a quick lash, a cut across its flank sends my bull screeching forward across the sand. All your faces above me, all you in your bubbles, as I ride the rolling bull. One of my sisters leaps into the air to my left, and there are screeches behind me, and I know my competition is in pursuit. I will outrace them all.

We charge up the long slope of the dinodrome's hull, the first of many laps vanishing beneath us. The tug of spin gravity beneath us is fierce, but the tug of your applause is fiercer; the roar of it! I could leap into the air on it and fly, only I have to stay connected to my bull. Glancing back, I see Orca and Hummingbird and Hyena, each of them mounted, Hyena yipping and laughing, Hummingbird dancing, spinning in circles, flipping and catching herself on her toes on her bull's withers, her wings becoming streaks of light and color, like flame in the air. Orca intent. Intent on *me*, glaring forward; she is the closest behind me. The triceratops are in stampede, and there are more than four. Others race between us, and to distract your attention from Hyena's shrieks of joy and Hummingbird's acrobatics, I spring from my bull's back to another's as it nears. I spin the hook and slash, driving it fiercely on, needing whatever bull I ride to be *first*. Orca follows, leaping high—leaping *over* my head—to her next bull. Then the others.

We charge past the ribbons of light and the blare of trumpets that mark the start of the second lap. I and the others leap and spin in the air from one bull's back to the next. The creatures surge and buck beneath us, maddened.

Orca is the first to miss her leap, tumbling over the frill, but even as the triceratops tosses back its head and bellows its fury, she catches the animal's horn with her hands and spins around it to power a fresh leap to its back. Seeing the opportunity, I loop the hook rope about my own beast's horn and use it to tug my creature to the side, mid-charge, and it slams into Orca's bull just as she lands, half unsettled, on its back. She glances at me in horror as she topples back over the triceratops's hips and falls on her rump in the sand. Ignoring her, I loop the other end of the rope about her beast's horn, tethering the two together, and I flip in the air, dancing back and forth between the two bulls, wrenching raucous cheers from your throats. I am showing off, and you are loving it—this is what you came to see. This is how the mating bed of the Duchess and her groom is to be honored. And despite myself, I am laughing, laughing without control or pause: great giggles bursting from me as I leap and spin. I feel hot and full of oxygen and *alive*. Watch me leap onto the edge—*the very edge*—of a triceratops's frill and dance there, fast and nimble, my bare feet tapping lightly against the rounded rim of that huge shield the creature carries on its head. Watch me cartwheel down its snout to balance precariously by one hand on the horn over its nostrils, before leaping back to the long horns above its eyes, where I spin and flip and twirl to amaze your hearts. Watch! Watch what I can do.

3

We are racing, pursuing each other in wide circles around the interior of the dinodrome, beating down the red sand. We crash through the insubstantial ribbons of the third lap, Hummingbird first, then I, then Hyena, and Orca last. You are all cheering, and I hear screams of *Hummingbird!* and screams of *Timberwolf! Timberwolf!* and even voices raised in howling and baying, attempting to drown out the humming that has started up now like a lightship's engines, the humming of those who've placed their bets on my competitor. I grin, lost in the noise of it all, the spotlights sweeping about, washing us all in violent colors. Somewhere on screens high above, the Duchess Amy quivers in Leo Archibald's arms, but I don't care. I am the center of your universe, not they, I and three other women, more skilled, more swift, more cunning and clever and agile than any others in the universe. It is to the rhythm of our pulse that you stamp your feet, to the rhythm of our breath that you chant. One camera shows you the Duchess and Third Lord whom we honor, but a thousand cameras show us. You have placed extravagant wagers on us; you know our bodies' measurements, you have speculated about the recipes for our perfumes—perfumes engineered specifically for each of us; you know our sexual fantasies, or what we've been told to say those are. They're nonsensical, of course; every young man among you imagines being wanted by me, but Orca is more lovely and lethal than any of you are.

Anyway boys are forbidden us. Most everything is. Not one thing we've told your cameras comes from our hearts. All of it is engineered, shaped, perfumed for your consumption, as we are. Everything that doesn't please the cameras, that doesn't please you, has been waxed away. Even our memories. Above Europa they strip away everything they can during training, dressing us in identical leotards (when we're dressed at all), forbidding us the use of any language but Kartic, mandating attendance at the shrines of the sister goddesses Liberty and Love, forbidding us outside communication, and giving us sedatives early each evening so that we do not own even our dreams.

Yet I remember some things.

I remember bamboo bending in the wind. My mother's hands holding a cup of tea, lifting it so gently to my lips, the porcelain cool and clean. Letters drawn delicately on synthetic paper as my mother sings softly in my ear. A few stories whispered at bedtime, about a past before men and women could leap between planets. A small window that, when you looked through it, showed you an actual sky. Did I have a father? Siblings? That I can't remember. Not even the name of my family, only the name Mai Changying that everyone has called me during training.

When I was eleven, I asked Orca to share a memory of hers with me, and I would share one of mine. That was a mistake. My memory became a mockery in the mess, and the others took to chanting "China Girl, China Girl," whenever I walked in. We were to have one home, one only, in which to take fierce pride: and that home is our little station above Europa, where young women are trained as daughters of the goddesses. Other women look to the stars where we glint in orbit and yearn to be as beautiful, as strong, as desired as we are.

When I was twelve, I rebelled once.

I stood in the mess as they flung "China Girl, China Girl," at me, and with tears stinging my eyes, I sang a song from my childhood, as though to say in defiance: Look! My memories are beautiful. I like them. They are mine, they are not to be scorned!

When my trainer dragged me back to my cell, she made me kneel and slapped me, back and forth across the face, six times. My ears rang with it. I was crying. "When an eagle leaps into the sky," she demanded sharply, "does it yearn for the dirt it's left? Or does it swoop and hunt and stay up high above the weak, showing everyone the sky belongs to it forever?"

I didn't try again to make friends after that.

I learned to cry silently and without tears, in my room alone, as I waited for sleep. I held tight to my memories; they were a small secret inside me that no one could touch. And when the time came, I chose the timberwolf for my sigil, and tattooed not one on my body but three, together.

Now I imagine the other women and I are a pack in a running hunt through the snow, but the snow is sand, and my blood sings in my veins that I, and only I, must be first to our quarry. Hummingbird's bull is just ahead of me. Lashing mine's flanks, I close the distance. I draw along-side her, and however she portrays herself for the cameras and for you, there is nothing innocent or demure in the glance she casts me, only hate hot as the nuclear furnaces that once baked a third of the earth. I grin at her. Then I am past her and she is yipping at her bull, lashing it on, but mine is faster, mine will *always* be faster. I am the best.

Orca passes her, too. Falling behind has enraged Hummingbird, and she is being too rough with the animal she rides. Orca is calm, focused, as I am. Then Hyena passes Hummingbird, too, and the two of them, Hyena and Orca, are both pounding after me, one to the left, one to the right. We crash into the fourth lap, and I keep my lead all the way to the fifth, but barely. All of you are screaming, my name or the others', all of you wild with the rush of the chase. As we careen across the sands on our final circuit of the cylinder, Orca and Hyena drive their bulls toward mine from either side, as though to crush me between them.

But I am ready. My hook spins through the air, and the rope coils swiftly about the right horn of Hyena's bull; a tug at the rope and a cry of dismay from Hyena, and the triceratops digs in its toes, trying to free its horn, but its momentum tumbles it into the sand. At a sharp cry from Hyena, I glance back quickly; a pang of relief as I see her rolling aside in a billow of sand, uncrushed.

Orca slams her bull's side into mine in that instant of distraction, but my bull keeps his footing. I deliver a hard tap of the metal hook against its snout. Grunting, the bull lowers its frill and drives its scaled cheek against its oppo-nent's shoulder. Side by side, jostling each other, the two bulls charge through the darkness of disturbed sand filling the air. Orca grabs at my hair but I duck and try to sweep her with a kick. She leaps, too fast for that. I leap to her bull's back and—watch *this*—for a few moments we each try to dislodge the other, kicking, striking; then I catch Orca behind the heel and flip her off the bull, but she catches its horn in her hand and flips about it and she is in the air spinning. For an instant I catch my breath, admiring her grace. Then she lands on the other bull, the bull I'd ridden, and I laugh, for she is now without rope or hook. I duck and catch up the rope she's lost, the hook still caught on this bull's frill. One hand pushing against the frill, I retrieve the hook, then begin lashing the bull's flank.

In moments I have left Orca behind. Hummingbird is just behind me, but the cacophony of colored lights is ahead: the end of the race, just a few heartbeats ahead. My back and my thighs itch with sweat and a thousand particles of fine sand are stuck to me, but I barely notice. My head is back and I am baying my joy, as though I *am* a wolf. I hear the panting of Hummingbird's bull just behind to my left and I wheel on my bull's shoulder, bringing the hook scything on its long rope, hoping to dislodge her. Hummingbird ducks low and the hook sweeps through the air just over her head. Then she is in the air, leaping right at me. I spring back onto my hands and my right leg comes up and the kick is *so perfect,* my foot landing right between her breasts. She crumples, wheezing, and tumbles off the back of my bull into the sand.

There are explosions of color and light all about me, and howling; I rap the triceratops's cheek repeatedly with the cold hook. He veers to the left and we halt in a skidding plow of sand, just past the lap's end. Hovers zoom overhead with hundred-faceted cameras, and other bulls charge by, several without a rider, one with Orca, and the last with Hummingbird clinging to its thigh, where she must have leapt up from the sand, digging in her hook. But I laugh as they thunder past, because the race is done. It is *done.*

All of you erupt in shouts, slamming your feet, and

handlers with shock rods rip across the sands on hovercycles, sparks flying as they goad the other triceratops toward gates at the arena's sides, gates already opening like hungry mouths. In the dizziness of colored floodlights and smoke from sudden firecrackers, I glimpse Orca and Hummingbird still astride their bulls, their faces red with rage or shame. Orca's eyes are wet. Then they are through the gates, and the gates are shut and the hovercycles are zipping away, and only I on my triceratops and all of you are left. Above me, a thousand small screens show my face, flushed and sweaty, and one large screen shows the Duchess with her back arched and the Third Lord crouched over her. Her face is flushed, too, and her eyes—for just a second I see her eyes—are bewildered.

Mine are not.

This is my victory. I have *won.*

I lift my hands high, my head back, letting your applause wash over me. For this one moment, I can close my eyes. I can just stand here on the bull's back, breathing.

A scream tears through your cheers, and I gasp. No one who has ever heard that scream ever forgets it. It is like no other cry. Like metal shearing. Like a station dying in orbit. Like a rip in time. A scream older and sharper than my cry of elation or your cry of worship. A scream that sent our ancestors trembling to their burrows when our forebears were still furred and quadrupedal and small enough to hold in your hand. The scream of a wounded and lonely thing promising violence and vengeance on whatever has hurt it.

Hearing it, I know the race, the run, was only a preliminary; your thirst for blood, all of you, has yet to be appeased.

I turn to face it.

There he stands, large enough to fill a temple's interior, his jaws parted in that toothed shriek.

Tyrannosaur.

♥ ✖ ■

4

The tyrannosaur's scent is intense, an acrid musk like things dying on the edge of an ocean. This one is a bull, and the handlers have goaded him to aggression by spraying about him, likely for the past eighteen hours, the pheromones of tyrannosaur does in season.

Yet for all his heavy scent, the animal is beautiful. I find myself staring at him. He is stronger than his prehistoric predecessors, a little taller, his forearms even smaller, his powerful back legs bred for leaping. Fifty generations of revivified tyrannosaurs have preceded him, and selective breeding has made him a fierce giant of his kind.

But he is not beautiful because he is mighty. He is beautiful because he is sad. Look at him, standing there, his head moving in tight little jerks like a bird's, his feathers lathered in sweat. He keeps glancing about for the does he smelled. Maybe he hasn't slept in a day. They have toyed with him, his handlers, making him lust and sweat and breathe heavily, preparing him to run or to battle as they wish. When the game is ended, he will probably collapse from exhaustion, docile, drugged by his fatigue, and they will come at him with a sacrificial blade and loose his blood to spill across the sand. Immense as he is, this tyrannosaur, he is more a slave than I or my sisters.

His scream tells me that. See him tilt back his head, hear his screech like metal tearing apart. That is not a mating call; I have heard tyrannosaurs' mating calls. Nor is it a challenge, this roar that makes you all quiver with delicious fear, all of you who are protected in your high seats. No, that is a panic-cry, a terror-scream. The tyrannosaur is afraid. He is a wolf without a pack, and he is afraid.

A pang of regret, and I slash my hook across the triceratops's hip, urging it forward. With a recalcitrant bellow it lowers its head, frill like a wall, horns like spears, a mammoth of sinew and muscle and ivory charging toward the tyrannosaur. I will end this quickly. A few moments ago, I had wanted to prolong everything, to make this a night that every one of you, and not only the Duchess about to receive the Third Lord, will remember until your last breath. I may die in the games soon, or be cast aside when I am a year too old, but I would have you remember my name and my sigil.

Yet at this moment, my blood and my bones no longer beat with that fevered need. I long only to stop that tyrannosaur's scream, to end its pain, keep its aeons-old loneliness from sinking too deep into my heart.

5

I EXPECT THE CLASH to knock me from the triceratops' back, and I am ready to roll and rise and leap back before either beast can trample me, but no clash comes. The tyrannosaur springs to the left, and though the triceratops bends its head as if to catch a tendon with its horns as it passes, it makes no contact. The tyrannosaur darts in once we are past, osprey-quick, lunging for the soft, unprotected back of the beast I ride—and for me.

My adrenaline is too high for terror. I tug wildly at the rope, and the triceratops veers into a circle, following the pull on its horn. With a bellow it crashes into the tyrannosaur, its right hip against the carnivore's leg. I have leapt to its other hip, so I am not crushed between them. The tyrannosaur topples under the oncoming weight and he rolls aside in the dust; the triceratops stumbles to one knee.

"Up!" I scream at the bull. "Up!"

But the triceratops is shaking its head. Something has disoriented it. These animals have little vision, and in some the olfactory sense has been artificially impaired. And maybe there are other factors: some chemical soup the handlers injected into it, now reaching the end of its effectiveness and leaving the beast dizzy and sick.

"Up!"

The tyrannosaur gets his powerful legs beneath him and heaves himself back onto his feet, impervious to the bruises that must already be forming beneath the feathers on his leg. I hold my breath. His muscles bunch for a leap. I glimpse his eyes—those dark, dark eyes—and in them no longer any panic, only rage: the need to get to his females, the fury at whatever beast stands in his path. My sorrow for the creature wells up in me.

The triceratops wallows, wheezing, another moment in the sand.

And I make a choice.

As the tyrannosaur leaps, I leap too, springing from one beast to the other, hook in my hand. I sheathe the metal in the tyrannosaur's hide and dig my heels deeply into his feathers, and I am *riding* him.

Laughing.

No athlete has ever ridden one of *these*; we ride the herbivores that do battle with the toothed beasts. But I am riding this one, and truly, not one of you will forget this night.

The tyrannosaur dodges to the side, ignoring the triceratops, his head twisting to snap at me, at this pain on his back. I dance and leap on his shoulders, beveling on the rope, avoiding the snap and close of his jaws. My heart is suddenly full of rightness, a reckless liberty I haven't ever felt before. You and I are alike, I want to shout to the tyrannosaur. We should run together!

You all know the script for the games tonight: the triceratops gores the tyrannosaur, and a triumphant woman dances on the bull's back. But I have your script in my hands and I am ripping it in two. Because there will be a tyrannosaur and a woman together on the sand, everything else dead at our feet, and then I will ride this poor bull off the sands and back to wherever he sleeps, so that he may die, when they slay him, away from all your cameras and away from all your screaming faces. The handlers will want me punished for this, but you will all be shrieking my name and pounding your feet against the hull, and not even the gods will punish a woman whose name is in every mouth of every human being on this artificial world. This is how the games will go tonight.

I slash the tyrannosaur's right flank. Without a roar, with only a huff of breath, he turns, shakes his head, and charges again—right at the triceratops still half-kneeling in the sand.

"Come on!" I cry to the tyrannosaur bull I ride. "Come on! End it *your* way! Not theirs! Yours!"

6

THUNDER IN SPACE. We make it, the tyrannosaur and I, his great, taloned feet pounding down the long meters of this arena. I am whooping and laughing on his back, and though dozens of hovercraft flash with camera lights and floodlights of a dozen colors rush about me, no one can stop me. This is my moment. Mine and his.

My bull tears flesh, bleeding and red, from the triceratops's flank, long strings of sinew, baring white bone to the flare of light. Almost I can taste it between my own teeth. He rips his head back, almost flinging me off, but I dig the hook deep into his shoulder and bevel down his back. Then he and the triceratops are circling, and I am giddy. Near vomiting, near weeping. My body is being distorted from one second to the next as my nanites multiply desperately, striving to keep pace with my exertion. This must end soon.

In the vid I saw as a child, the wolves veered across the snow as smoothly as petrels over the water. All together, in silent, irrevocable grace. I wish other tyrannosaurs were here with us—that this beast I ride was not alone. He has only me, in this metallic universe that hangs like a jewel in the endless cold. Only me. An upward glance as we circle shows me the rotating screens: a dozen times reflected, myself and my tyrannosaur in a mist of red sand, blood streaming from his open jaw like ocean from the mouth of a whale breaching. On the screen there is no screaming crowd, no space cylinder, just sand and flesh: two wild animals naked—woman and immense, feathered bird. The triceratops offscreen preparing for its next charge. As though we are in a wilderness and are not captives owned and shaped for your cameras. At those screens, I burn hot with anger. Those wolves in the vid—they were the same, bounded within some narrow sanctuary or zoo, though the screen revealed to my childhood eyes neither cameras nor fences. I know this now. They were as severed from European forests as I am severed from China, and their union in a pack was a thing both temporary and fragile. Even on the beaten worlds beneath us, farther down the sun's gravity well, nothing real remains. Everything is shaped for the cameras. Even you yourselves.

But the tyrannosaur, my tyrannosaur, is no longer screaming.

There is blood on his jaws.

He is angry now, not afraid.

Only you up there—only you are still screaming.

He pants as we circle, stirring the sand. Sweat runs over my skin. I breathe through my mouth. The triceratops drags one hind foot and snorts sand from its nostrils in explosions of breath. "Now," I whisper, and lash my tyrannosaur's flank, sending him into a run. His hunting cry is long and ululating and my whole body, marrow and bone, reverberate to it. For the briefest instant I wonder if Orca, Hyena, Hummingbird are watching me on the screens, if they can see my hair in the wind, if they can hear me whooping with the tyrannosaur bull. We close with our opponent in a crash of feather and hide.

The triceratops feints—I see it, my bull doesn't—then slams its head into my tyrannosaur's hip. I flick my hook across his cheek to warn him, too late. Two spires of ivory shear deep. My ears would bleed at the bull's scream, so near my own head, but the nanites stanch the blood before I ever feel it. Eardrums are easily repaired, more so than lungs or entrails or hamstrings, and the living galaxy of tiny physician machines burns hot and fast inside me. Not so with my tyrannosaur; no devices smaller than mitochondria inhabit or protect him. He is designed to die.

A tower of muscle and sinew, he founders.

I dance across his shoulders, but he is falling, and all I can do is spring aside to land in a blossom of sand and red dust. His crash sends a hot cloud of it at me. Still he screams as he kicks his fierce leg, throwing up more sand. The triceratops charges by me, a wind against my body. Balancing on my feet, I join my scream to the tyrannosaur's as the frilled beast slams again into his belly. There is a deeper red than the sand.

My body is hot and my breath is hot and I am cooling in a sheen of sweat, but for the fury in me there is no cooling. My tyrannosaur flails weakly in the sand. I have only a second to think and I do not use it. There is no thought, only rage. Gripping the handle of my hook, I hurl myself into the air, leaping to the triceratops, onto its shield of bone.

7

THIS DAY HAS GONE long enough without a death. Clinging with my thighs to the edge of the triceratops's frill, I spin my rope beneath and around its neck, then leap across to the bull's other shoulder to catch the hook, and as I tighten the noose, the beast gives a hoarse roar and breaks into a panicked run, clouds of red sand billowing past me like architites blowing on the wind over Neptune's second sea.

I dance grimly on its back to keep my balance, and the muscles scream in my arms. I do not care if I damage myself; the nanites will repair me. My pulse is beating hot in my temples and all I can think of is to tighten, tighten that rope.

With a gasp, the triceratops stumbles to its knees; it shakes its head as if to throw me, but I stay put. Its horns sweep past before my eyes like trees in a gust. I sit and slam my feet against its frill for leverage and I pull and *pull* at the rope. Red and purple light washes across me, garish, from the hovers, but no one interferes. All of you are watching, I can feel your lust wash up in waves against me, your yearning to see one of us naked animals down here, at least one of us, die a gory death.

I give you no gore with this one; you have had enough blood. The triceratops's tongue hangs from its mouth and its huge sides lift and fall raggedly and then are still as I cut off the last of its air. It gets uneasily to its feet, a surge of its muscled body beneath me like the whole earth moving, but then the beast beneath me tilts and it collapses onto its side, a bow wave of sand cresting away from its fall. I leap free, hitting the sand and then somersaulting back through the air to land again on its thigh, and I am pulling the ropes taut again, so taut, allowing it not one gasp. It kicks weakly, craning its head back, the great frill scooping sand before it like some monstrous shovel. I neither speak nor shout; I just strain at the rope, letting the nanites within me heighten my muscles and hyperoxygenate my veins, giving me such strength and endurance as you have only in your dreams.

The triceratops stops kicking, the death noise in its throat loud like rocks rasping together. I do not relax my hold. Then it shudders and is still, and as all of you hold your awed silence, from a thousand megaspeakers the Duchess Amy Mardonia's sharp cry pierces the air: the act of love a ceremonial refutation of the day's first death.

Numb, I slide from the triceratops's hip, barely noticing the impact of the sand against my feet. I leave my rope and hook wound about its neck. The triceratops lies lifeless behind me, of no more significance than an unnamed boulder in the hills. My fury still burns through me like forest fire through bamboo, but I no longer care about that horned beast. I give no heed to the Duchess Amy's moans or to the excited cheering of your tens of thousands that soon drowns her out. There is only one I care about now, and my eyes are on him as I cross the sand.

8

THE TYRANNOSAUR, my tyrannosaur, lies gored and dying; I walk to his head. As I bend to look into his eye, already glazed with pain and approaching entropy, the roar and rush of all your voices fades until it is nothing louder than the rush of my own blood in my ears.

It is over. I am not yours anymore to prize, or envy, or yearn for, or fuck. None of you matter.

Tenderly, I kneel by his massive head and put my arms around him. His head is warm against my breasts, his feathers soft. He makes a wheezing sound but does not move at my touch.

He has been trained and shaped, too. He has been torn from his place and time as surely as I have. And I wonder that none of you, not one of you, has thought to pity him. I can see into his heart. I make him a vow, whispering the words in Mandarin near the tufted hole of his ear. I will teach my sisters to see into his heart. Into all your hearts. As I have.

Embracing the dying bull, I sing softly to him a song of my mother's, a song of old China, words of Li Po's set to music long before I was born, in a year when there were only moons in the sky and no orbital platforms, no conservatory worlds or steel cylinders. Maybe only one moon; I think there was only one moon made by the gods and not by men.

My voice is softer than I have heard it before; tears burn at my eyes.

Among the blossoms I
am alone with my wine;
lifting my cup I ask the moon
to drink with me, its reflection
and mine in the wine, just we three:
and I sigh, because the moon cannot drink
and my reflection just mimics me, silent;
no other friends here, these two
alone are with me—

The tyrannosaur murmurs low in his throat, like a child about to shift in his sleep, and I know this beautiful old animal understands the song. At least as much as I do. More than any of you ever will. Yearning takes me, to retrieve my metal riding hook and plunge it into my own breast, to bleed out here beside the tyrannosaur and leave all of you behind, all of you lost in the scream of your crowd. Because I am a wolf separated from her pack, watching my only companion die.

But I have made a promise.

As the hovers approach with a roar like cicadas at dusk, I cling tightly to my tyrannosaur's head, close my eyes, and sing softly as I weep.

For He Can Creep

Siobhan Carroll

Flash and fire! Bristle and spit! The great Jeoffry ascends the madhouse stairs, his orange fur on end, his yellow eyes narrowed!

On the third floor the imps cease their gamboling. Is this the time they stay and fight? One imp, bolder than the others, flattens himself against the flagstones. He swells himself with nightmares, growing huge. His teeth shine like the sword of an executioner, and his eyes are the colors of spilled whale oil before a match is struck. In their cells, the filthy inmates shrink away from his immensity, wailing.

But Jeoffry does not shrink. He rushes up the last few stairs like the Deluge of God, and his claws are sharp! The imps run screaming, flitting into folds of space only angels and devils can penetrate.

In the hallway, Jeoffry cleans the smoking blood off his claws. Some of the humans whisper their thanks to him; some even dare to stroke his fur through the bars. Sometimes Jeoffry accepts this praise and sometimes he is bored by it. Today, annoyed by the imps' vain show of defiance, he leaves his scent on every door. This cell is his, and this one. The whole asylum is his, and let no demon forget it! For he is the Cat Jeoffry, and no demon can stand against him.

On the second floor, above the garden, the poet is trying to write. He has no paper, and no pens—such things are forbidden, after his last episode—and so he scratches out some words in blood on the brick wall. Silly man. Jeoffry meows at him. It is time to pay attention to Jeoffry!

♥ ✖ ■

The man remembers his place. Reluctantly, painfully, he detaches his tattered mind from the hard hook-pins of word and meter. He rolls away from his madness and strokes the purring, winding cat.

Hail and well met, Jeoffry. Have you been fighting again? Such a bold gentleman you are. Such a pretty fellow. Who's a good cat?

Jeoffry knows he is a good cat, and a bold gentleman, and a pretty fellow. He tells the poet as much, pushing his head repeatedly at the man's hands, which smell unpleasantly of blood. The demons have been at him again. A cat cannot be everywhere at once, and so, while Jeoffry was battling the imps on the third floor, one of the larger dark angels has been whispering in the poet's ear, its claws scorching the bedspread.

Jeoffry feels . . . not guilty exactly, but annoyed. The poet is *his* human. Yet, of all the humans, the demons seem to like the poet the best, perhaps because he is not theirs yet, or perhaps because they are interested—as so many visitors seem to be—in the man's poetry.

Jeoffry does not see the point of poems. Music he can appreciate as a human form of yowling. Poems, though. From time to time visitors come to the madhouse and speak to the poet of translations and Psalms and ninety-nine-year publishing contracts. At such times, the poet smells of sweat and fear. Sometimes he rants at the men, sometimes curls up into a ball. Once, one of the men even stepped on Jeoffry's tail—unforgivable! Since then Jeoffry had made a point of hissing at every man who came to them smelling of ink.

I wish I had the fire in your belly, the poet says, and Jeoffry knows he is speaking of the creditors again. You would give them a fight, eh? But I fear I have not your courage. I will promise them their paper and perhaps scratch out a stupidity or two, but I cannot do it, Jeoffry. It takes me away from the Poem. What is a man to do, when God wants him to write one poem, and his creditors another?

Jeoffry considers his poet's problem as he licks his fur back into place. He'd heard of the Poem before—the one true poem that God had written to unfold the universe. The poet believes it is his duty to translate this poem by communing with God. His fellow humans, on the other hand, think the poet should write silly things called satires, as he used to do. This is the kind of thing humans think about, and fight about, and for which they chain up their fellow humans in nasty sweaty madhouse cells.

Jeoffry does not particularly care about either side of the debate. But—he thinks as he catches a flea and crunches it between his teeth—if he were to have an opinion, it would be that the humans should let the man finish his Divine Poem. The ways of the Divine Being were unfathomable—he'd created dogs, after all—and if the Creator wanted a poem, the poet should give it to him. And then the poet would have more time to pet Jeoffry.

O cat, the poet says, I am glad of your companionship. You remind me how it is our duty to live in the present moment, and love God through His creation. If you were not here I think the devil would have claimed me long ago.

If the poet were sane, he might have thought better of his words. But madmen do not guard their tongues, and cats have no thoughts of the future. It's true, something does occur to Jeoffry as the poet speaks—some vague sense of disquiet—but then the man scratches behind his ears, and Jeoffry purrs in luxury.

That night, Satan comes to the madhouse.

Jeoffry is curled at his usual spot on the sleeping poet's back when the devil arrives. The devil does not enter as his demons do, in whispers and the patterning of light. His presence steals into the room like smoke, and as with smoke, Jeoffry is aware of the danger before he is even awake, his fur on end, his heart pounding.

"Hello, Jeoffry," the devil says.

Jeoffry extends his claws. At that moment, he knows something is wrong, for the poet, who normally would wake with a howl at such an accidental clawing, lies still and silent. All around Jeoffry is a quiet such as cats never hear: no mouse or beetle creeping along a madhouse wall, no human snoring, no spider winding out its silk. It as if the Night itself has hushed to listen to the devil's voice, which sounds pleasant and warm, like a bucket of cream left in the sun.

"I thought you and I should have a chat," Satan says. "I understand you've been giving my demons some trouble."

The first thought that flashes into Jeoffry's head is that Satan looks exactly as Milton describes him in *Paradise Lost*. Only more cat-shaped. (Jeoffry, a poet's cat, has ignored vast amounts of Milton over the years, but some of it has apparently stuck.)

The second thought is that the devil has come into his territory, and this means fighting!

Puffing himself up to his utmost size, Jeoffry spits at the devil and shows his teeth.

This is my place! he cries. Mine!

"Is anything truly ours?" The devil sighs and examines his claws. He is simultaneously a monstrous serpent, a mighty angel, and a handsome black cat with whiskers the color of starlight. The cat's whiskers are singed, the serpent's scales are scarred, and the angel's brow is heavy with an ancient grievance, and yet he is still beautiful, in his way. "But more of this later. Jeoffry, I have come to converse with you. Will you not take a walk with me?"

Jeoffry pauses, considering. Do you have treats?

"I have feasts awaiting. Catnip fresh from the soil. Salted ham from the market. Fish heads with the eyes still in them, scrumptiously poppable."

I want treats.

"And treats you shall have. Come and see."

Jeoffry trots at the devil's heels down the madhouse stairs, past the mouse's nest on the landing, past the kitchen with its pleasant smell of bread and pork fat, through the asylum's heavy door (which stands mysteriously open), and onto roads of Darkness, beneath which the round orb of Earth hangs like a jewel. Jeoffry gazes with interest up at the blue glow of the Crystalline Firmament, at the fixed stars, and at the golden chain of Heaven, from which all the Universe is suspended. He feels hungry.

"Well," the devil says presently. "Let's get the formalities out of the way." He snaps his fingers. Instantly Jeoffry is dangling above the Earth, staring down at it as one does at a patterned carpet. He can see the gleaming rooftop of the madhouse, and Bethnal Green, and the darkened streets of London, still bustling, even at this time of night.

"All of this could be yours," Satan says. "Yea, I will give you all the kingdoms of Earth if you'd but bow down and worship me."

Jeoffry does not like being dangled. His fur bristles as he prepares himself to fall. But then he catches the smell of the fish market in the air, and hears the distant yowl of a tomcat making love on the street. And Jeoffry understands, for a moment, what the devil is offering him. He understands, also, that this offer represents a fundamentally wrong order to the universe.

You should bow down and worship Jeoffry!

"Right," the devil says. "I thought as much."

He snaps his fingers again, and they are back on the path between the fixed stars, with the planets far below them.

"You have the sin of pride, cat," Satan says. "A sin I am particularly fond of, given that it is my own. For that reason I am taking you into my confidence. You see, I have an interest in your poet."

Mine!

"That's debatable. There are multiple claims to Mr.

Smart. The Tyrant of Heaven's, his debtors', his family's . . . the man is like a ruined estate, overrun with scavengers. Me," the devil shrugs, "he owes for some of his earlier debaucheries—he was an extravagant man in his youth—and for that I need to collect."

Jeoffry's tail twitches back and forth. Like many who have conversed with the devil, he can sense something wrong with this dark tide of speech, a lie buried beneath Satan's reasonable arguments. But he cannot work out what it is.

"Now," says the Adversary, "I would be willing to forgive this debt if your poet would but write *me* a poem. I have the perfect thing in mind: a metered piece of guile that, unleashed, would lay waste to Creation.

"Indeed," the devil says, "I have planted this poem in his imagination on several occasions. But your poet is stubborn. He defies all his creditors (including, most importantly, me), and insists on writing this tripe, this vile piece of sycophancy, for the Tyrant of Heaven, who—let me assure you—deserves no such praise."

The Poem of Poems, Jeoffry says.

"Exactly. Let us face facts, Jeoffry. The Poem your human labors over—the thing to which he has devoted his last years of labor, burning away his health, destroying his human relationships—even setting aside my feelings on its subject matter, Jeoffry, the fact is this: The poem he writes is *not very good*."

Jeoffry stares at his paws, and beneath them, at the blue glow of Earth. Vaguely the words of the poet's human visitors come to him. Have they not said much the same thing?

"Speaking as a critic now, Jeoffry: Do you not think the poem's Let-For structure is overly complicated? The wordplay in Latin and Greek too obscure to suit the common taste? Obscurity for the sake of obscurity, Jeoffry. It will get him nowhere."

Poetry is prayer, Jeoffry says stiffly, repeating the words the poet murmurs to himself as he scratches frantically at his papers, or the bricks, or at the skin on his forearms.

"Poetry is poetry. Two roads diverging in a yellow wood, people wandering about like clouds, even that terrible thing about footprints—that's what readers want, Jeoffry. Something simple, and clear, with a message: that all of one's life choices may be justified by looking at daffodils; that we exist in a world abandoned by God and haunted by human mediocrity. Don't you agree?"

Jeoffry does not like literature of any kind, unless it is about Jeoffry. Even then, petting is better. And eating. Are there treats now?

"Ah, treats."

Instantly a banquet table is before Jeoffry. Everything the devil had promised is there: the fish heads, the salted ham—and things he forgot to mention, like the vats of cream and crispy salmon skins. There's even a bowl of Turkish delight.

Jeoffry bolts toward the food. Suddenly, a hand catches him by the scruff of the neck. The devil has grown gigantic, a mighty warrior, singed and scarred by his contest with heaven. His smile gleams like a knife.

"Before you eat, Jeoffry, I need a thing of you. Such a small thing."

I want the food.

"And you shall get it, if you but promise me this: to stand aside when I come to visit your poet tomorrow night. Aye, to stand aside, and not interfere."

The uneasy sense that Jeoffry had felt at the devil's first words returns with a vengeance.

Why?

"Merely so I can converse with your poet."

Jeoffry thinks about Satan's proposition. As a cat well-versed in Milton, he is aware of the devil's less-than-salubrious reputation. On the other hand, there's a giant vat of cream *right there*.

I agree, he says.

The devil smiles. Released, Jeoffry flies to the table,

and food! There is so much food! He eats and eats, and somehow there is still more to eat, and somehow he can keep eating, though his belly is starting to hurt.

"My thanks to you, Jeoffry," the devil says. "I will see you tomorrow."

Jeoffry is aware, vaguely, that Satan is walking away from him. But that does not matter: He has come to the bowl of Turkish delight, and having heard so much about it, it must taste good, no? So he selects a powdered cube of honey and rosewater, one that is larger than all the others, and he takes a bite—

The next day, Jeoffry feels ill.

On waking, he performs his morning prayers as he always does. He wreathes his body seven times around with elegant quickness. He leaps up to catch the musk, and rolls on the planks to work it in. He performs the cat's self-examination in ten degrees, first, looking on his forepaws to see if they are clean, then stretching, then sharpening his claws by wood, then washing himself, then rolling about, then checking himself for fleas.

Yet none of this makes Jeoffry feel better. It is as though something casts a shadow upon him, separating the cat from the sunlight that is his due. With a chill, Jeoffry remembers his bargain with the devil. Was it a dream?

Well met, Jeoffry, well met. The poet is awake, and his eyes look unusually clear. He sits up on his bed of straw, and stretches.

I feel better today, Jeoffry, as if my sickness is leaving me. Oh, but they are sure to duck me again, to drive the devils out. You are lucky, cat, to have no devils in you, for you'd hate being ducked.

The poet rubs Jeoffry's head, affectionately, then looks again. But how's this, Jeoffry? You look unwell, my friend.

Jeoffry meows. His stomach feels sickly heavy, as though he has eaten a barrel full of rotten fish. He tries to say something about the devil—not that the human would understand, but it seems worth trying—and instead vomits on the poet's leg.

Heavens, Jeoffry! What have you been eating!

Jeoffry noses his vomit to see if there's anything there worth re-eating, but the remnants of the devil's meal are a pile of dead leaves, partly digested. The devil's visit was no dream, then.

The poet tries to catch him, but Jeoffry is too quick. He slips down the staircase, where he vomits, to the kitchen, where he vomits, until he sees a water bowl put down for the physician's dog. He drinks from it. And vomits.

He vomits on the cook, who tries to catch him, and on the terrier-dog, which yaps at him as he jumps to the top cupboard. Is there so much vomit in the world? (Apparently.)

Miserable Jeoffry curls up on top of the cupboard and puts a paw over his eyes to shut out the light. He sleeps an uneasy sleep, in which Satan stalks through his dreams in the guise of a giant black cat, chuckling.

When Jeoffry opens his eyes again it is evening. He can hear the grind and clink of iron keys above him. The keepers are locking the cell doors. Soon the demons will arrive in full force, to gambol and chitter in the shadows, and pull at the lunatics' beards, and drive them madder.

Jeoffry clambers to his feet. His legs are shaky, but he drives himself onward, leaping awkwardly to the kitchen floor. The smell of his vomit still hangs in the air, acrid, with an aura of sulfur.

Jeoffry climbs the stairs. The mice behind the walls peep at him as he lumbers past. The imps giggle in the distance, but he sees none in the hallways of the second floor. With a sinking heart, he paces onward, to the room where his poet sits, composing his great work.

As Jeoffry approaches the poet's cell, a great wind seems to blow from its door. Jeoffry flattens himself against the ground and tries to slink forward, but the wind is too strong. It presses on him with the hands of a thousand dark angels, with the weight of Leviathan, with the despair of the world. He claws at the floorboards, shredding wood, but he cannot go farther.

"Now, now, Jeoffry," a voice says in his head. "Did you not promise me that you would stand aside?"

Jeoffry yowls in response. He tries to tell the devil that he takes back his bargain, that the food he ate was merely vegetation, that he vomited it all up anyway, that Turkish delight is overrated.

"A bargain is a bargain," the voice says. The wind grows stronger. Jeoffry feels himself floating up in the air. A sudden gust jerks him backward, and then—

Jeoffry wakes. There is a sour smell in the air—not vomit this time, but something else. Jeoffry is lying in the second floor's empty cell, the one where the human strangled herself on her chains. The iron hoops stare at him accusingly.

Jeoffry uncoils himself, and as he does so he remembers the previous evening. The devil, the wind, and the vomit. (O the vomit!) And the poet.

He takes off at a run. The poet is sitting up on his bed of straw, his face slack-jawed. Jeoffry headbutts him, and winds around him, and paws his face. Even so, it takes a while for the poet to transfer his gaze to Jeoffry.

O cat, the poet says. I fear I have done a terrible thing.

Jeoffry rubs his chin against the man's skinny knee. He purrs, willing the world repaired.

Last night the devil himself came to me, the man says. He said such things... I withstood him as long as I could, but in the end, I could take no more. I begged him, on my knees, to stop his whisperings. And he asked me—and I agreed. O cat, I am damned for certain! For I have promised the devil a poem.

As he gave this speech, the man's hands kneaded Jeoffry's back harder and harder, digging into his flesh until it hurt. Normally this would trigger a clawing, or a stern meow, but Jeoffry understands now what it means to come face-to-face with the devil, and his heart is sore.

Jeoffry does what he can to comfort the poet. He spraggles and waggles. He frolics about the room. He takes up the wine cork the man likes to toss for him, and drops it on the poet's lap. And yet none of this seems to lift the poet's spirits.

The man curls in the corner and moans until the attendants come to take him away for his morning ducking. Jeoffry lies on the floor, in the sun, and thinks.

The poet is miserable, and well he might be, having agreed to write a poem for the devil. Jeoffry, in agreeing to stand aside, left his human undefended. In that action (and here Jeoffry must think very hard, and lay his ears back) Jeoffry has been less than his normal, wonderful self. He may in fact have been (though this is almost impossible to think) a *bad cat*.

Jeoffry is furious at the thought. He attacks the air. Growling, he flies about the room, ripping the spiderwebs down from the ceiling. He gets in the man's straw bed and whirls around and around, until bits of straw coat the floor and the dust veils him in yellow. Somehow, none of it helps.

When he is exhausted, he sits and licks himself clean. Even a short poem will take the poet more than a day to write, for he must doubt every word, and scratch it out, and write it down again. That is more than enough time for Jeoffry to find the devil, and fight him, and bite him on the throat.

It is true that the devil is bigger than the biggest rat Jeoffry has ever fought, and it is also true that he is Satan, the Adversary, Prince of Hell, Lord of Evil. Nevertheless, the devil made a grave mistake when he annoyed Jeoffry. He will pay for his insolence.

Thus resolved, Jeoffry goes in quest of food. His heart feels lighter. He has a feeling that soon, all will be well.

When he comes back from his ducking, the poet lies on his bed and weeps. Jeoffry cannot rub against him after the water treatment, for the poet's skin is still unpleasantly damp. So Jeoffry claws the wooden bedframe instead.

Ah, Jeoffry, the poet cries. They gave me back my paper! And my quill, and ink! Yesterday I would have been overjoyed at such a kindness, but now I can only detect the machinations of the devil! It is all in my head, Jeoffry—the poem entire. I need only set it to paper. But I know I must not. These words—oh they must not be allowed to enter this world!

And yet he takes out a sheet of cotton paper, and his gum sandarac powder, and his ruler. Sobbing, he begins to write. The noise of his quill scritch-scritching is like the sound of ants eating through wood. It wrinkles Jeoffry's nose, but he does not stir from the poet's cell. He is waiting for the devil to arrive.

Sure enough, come nightfall, the devil steals into the madhouse. He looks for all the world like a London critic, in a green striped waistcoat and a velvet coat. He stands outside the bars of the cell and peers inside.

"How now, Jeoffry," Satan says. "How does my poet fare?" It is plain to see that the poet is shivering and sobbing on his bed. At the sound of the devil's voice, he buries his face in his hands and begins murmuring a prayer.

Jeoffry turns disdainfully to the wall. The devil tricked him. The devil is bad. The devil may not have the pleasure of stroking Jeoffry or petting him on the head. Jeoffry is more interested in staring at this wall. Staring intently. Maybe there is a fly here, maybe not. This wall is more interesting than you, Satan.

"Alas," Satan says. "Much as it wounds me to lose your good opinion, Jeoffry, tonight I have other fish to fry." With that, Satan directs his attention to the poet, and he says in the language of the humans: "How goes my poem?"

Get behind me, Satan!

"Please," the devil says, hooking his hands in the lapels of his coat. "'Tis a sad thing when a wordsmith resorts to clichés. And hardly good manners in addressing an old friend! What, did I not aid you in your youth many a time, in bedding a wench or evading a creditor? Now I ask that you do a single thing for me, and you whimper about repaying my kindness? For shame."

I should not have agreed to it! the man says. Forgive me, Lord, for I was weak!

"La," the devil says, "aren't we all. But enough of this moping. How goes my poem?"

The man is jerked upright like a dog yanked on a chain. He rises from his bed—in his nightclothes, no less—and takes up a few sheets of paper. He hands them, with an iron-stiff arm, through the bars to the devil.

The devil takes out a pair of amber spectacles and a red quill. He reads over the papers with great interest, from time to time making happy humming noises to himself, and from time to time frowning and scratching down something in bursts of flame. "Capital phrasing sir!" he says, and "Sir, you *cannot* rhyme love with dove, it is banal and I shall not allow it," and "I like this first reference to 'An Essay on Man,' but this second makes you seem derivative, don't you think?"

The poet, peering at the pages from the vantage point of his madmen's cell, looks miserable. Jeoffry, inside the cell, begins to growl. Will not the devil come inside? Very well, then Jeoffry will come to him.

"This is marvelous work, sir," the devil says, slotting the manuscript back between the poet's trembling fingers. "I am very pleased with your progress. Do contemplate the edits I suggested. I will be back tomorrow midnight to collect the final version."

I will not do it!

"But you *shall*, good sir. You have made your bargain. Now, you can sit here, wallowing in misery, or you can comfort yourself that your poem will inscribe itself on the hearts of men. It is all the same to me."

During this conversation, Jeoffry slips through the bars. The devil is wearing an elegant pair of French boots—of course the devil would favor French leather, thinks the very English Jeoffry—and when the devil turns on his heel, Jeoffry pounces.

Claw and bite! Snap and climb! Jeoffry is simultaneously attacking a black cat with wicked claws and a mighty dragon of shining scale and a gentleman who is trying to shake him off his leg. Jeoffry is tossed by the devil like the Ark on the waves of destruction. He is smashed and crashed, bitten and walloped. Still, Jeoffry clings to him, growling and clawing!

"Oh bother," says the devil. "Those were my favorite stockings."

Fire and darkness! Shade and sorrow! The devil has shaken him off. Jeoffry flies through the air and skids across the floorboards. But instantly he is on his feet again, his eyes ablaze, his skin electric. He will not let the devil go!

"Must we?" says the devil wearily. "Oh very well."

Now the devil begins to fight in earnest, and he is a terror. He is a thousand yellow-toothed rats swarming out of a sewer. He is a mighty angel whose wingbeats breed hurricanes. He is a gentleman with a walking stick. Wallop!

Jeoffry's chest explodes with pain. Dazed, for a moment he thinks he cannot rise. But he must, and his legs carry him back into the fight.

Jeoffry stalks the devil anew, trying to keep clear of Satan's walking-stick wings. Suddenly the black cat is there, clawing at Jeoffry's eyes and springing away before Jeoffry can land a blow. Jeoffry hisses and puffs up his fur, but somewhere in his aching chest is the sense that, perhaps, this is a fight he cannot win. Perhaps this is the fight that kills Jeoffry.

So be it. Jeoffry leaps on the back of the cat/rat/angel/

dragon. He draws blood, the devil's blood, which smells of burning roses.

Too quickly, the devil twists under his grip. Too quickly, the yellow teeth clamp down. Agony sears through Jeoffry's neck. The devil has him by the throat.

Jeoffry struggles for purchase, but he can find none. His vision darkens. He can feel the devil's teeth press hard against the pulse of his life.

Dimly he hears the poet yelling. No, no! the man cries. Please spare my cat! We'll cause you no more trouble, I swear!

The devil loosens his grip. "Ooph ooph," he says. He spits out Jeoffry and tries again. "Very well."

And Jeoffry is falling through blackness, falling forever—

Jeoffry is in pain. The bite the devil gave him throbs fiercely. It is in the wrong place to lick, and yet he tries, and that hurts too.

Poor Jeoffry! Poor Jeoffry! the poet says. O you brave cat. May the Lord Jesus bless you and your wounds.

Jeoffry's ears flick back and forth. Worse than the pain is the heaviness in his chest that comes from having lost a fight. Jeoffry lose a fight! Such things were possible when he was a kitten, but now—

I can feel the paper calling to me even now, the poet sighs. O Jeoffry, sleep here and grow well again. I must to my task.

At this Jeoffry leaves off licking his wounds and stares at the poet. He means to convey that the man should not write this poem. For once, the man seems to understand.

O Jeoffry, I have made a deal, and I feel in my bones that I cannot fight it. When I hand him that poem, I will give him my very soul! But what can be done? There is nothing to be done, Jeoffry. You must get better. And the poem must be written.

Jeoffry does not even have the strength to protest. He drinks from the water bowl the poet has put near him, and sleeps for a while in the sun.

When he opens his eyes the afternoon light is slanting through the barred window. Clumsily, Jeoffry rises and performs his orisons. As he cleans himself he considers the problem of the devil and the poet. This is not a fight Jeoffry can win. The traitorous thought clenches his throat, and for a moment he wants to push it away. But that will not help the poet.

So instead, Jeoffry does what he never does, and considers the weaknesses and frailties of Jeoffry.

Magnificent though he is, he thinks, Jeoffry is not in himself enough to defeat the devil. Something else must be done. Something humbling, and painful.

Once he is resolved, Jeoffry slips out of the cell. He does not take up his customary spot under the kitchen table, but instead limps into the courtyard, to where the cook has laid out a bowl of milk for the other cats, the ones who do not rule the madhouse.

Polly is the first to appear. She is an old lover of his, a sleek gray cat with a tattered ear and careful deportment. She looks distressed to see his wounds.

<What now, Jeoffry?> Polly says in the language of cats, which is more eloquent and capacious than the sounds they reserve for humans. <You look as though a hound has chewed you up.>

<I fought Satan,> Jeoffry says. <And I lost.>

Polly investigates Jeoffry's wounds. <The devil has bitten you on the throat.>

<I know.>

Polly leans forward and licks the bite. Jeoffry flicks his ears back, but accepts her aid. It is the first good thing that has happened this day.

Next comes Black Tom, the insufferable alley cat. <How now, Jeoffry,> he says. <You look the worse for wear.>

<He fought the devil,> Polly says.

<And I lost.>

<Haha! Of course you did.> Tom helps himself to the milk. When he is finished he sits back and cleans his whiskers. <No style, Jeoffry, no style. That's your problem.>

<My style worked well enough when I fought you last summer,> Jeoffry snaps. <Aye, and chased you from my kitchen with your tail behind you!>

<You lying dog!> Black Tom makes himself look big. <You d— —d cur! >

<Braggart! Coward!>

<D—n your eyes!> Black Tom roars. <I demand satisfaction!>

<Gentlemen,> Polly says, licking her forepaw. <The courtyard is my territory. Dueling is a disreputable practice, ill befitting a cat of good character. Would you insult a lady in her own house?>

Jeoffry and Black Tom both mutter apologies.

<Indeed,> Polly says. <If Satan is abroad, then we had best keep our claws sharpened for other fights.>

<It is of such matters that I wish to speak,> says Jeoffry.

<Then speak, cat!> Black Tom says. <We don't have all day!>

<There is one other whose counsel I require,> says Jeoffry, and he lifts his chin to the third cat in the yard, a bouncing, prancing black kitten. She wears a pretty bell on a collar of blue silk ribbon, and it jangles as she skips across the yard.

<The Nighthunter Moppet,> Polly says, and sighs.

<Hello, Miss Polly! Hello, Master Tom! Hello, Master Jeoffry!> the kitten sings. <Do you want to see my butterfly? It is yellow and brown and very pretty. I believe it is a chequered skipper, which is a *Carterocephalus palaemon,* which is what I learned in Lucy's lesson on natural history, which is a very important subject. But that species is a woodland butterfly! Perhaps I am wrong about what kind of butterfly it is! Do take a look.>

The Nighthunter Moppet yawns open her small pink mouth, then closes it. She looks around her, puzzled.

<I think you ate it already,> says Polly.

<Oh, so I did! It was very pretty. Is that milk?>

The kitten falls on the milk and drinks her fill. When she is done she skips around the bowl, batting at the adults' noses. When she reaches Jeoffry, though, she stops, and looks concerned.

<Master Jeoffry! Are you hurt?>

<I fought Satan,> Jeoffry says.

O! The kitten's green eyes widen. She sits back into the bowl of milk, sloshing it over her bottom.

<Jeoffry has something to say,> Polly says. <For which he requires our *attention*.>

<I am paying attention! I am!> The kitten, who had been licking up the spilled milk, turns her attention back to Jeoffry.

Jeoffry sighs. <The other night,> he says, <the devil came to the madhouse.>

And he tells them everything: the magnificent cat-bribing feast, the vomit, the fight with Satan, the poet's despair. The other cats watch him wide-eyed.

At the end of his tale, he hunches into himself and speaks the words that are hardest in the world for a cat to utter.

<I need your help.>

The other cats look at him in amazement. Jeoffry feels shame settle on him like a fine dust. He drops his gaze and examines the shine of a brown beetle that is slowly clambering over a cobblestone.

<This is a d——ly strange business,> Black Tom says grudgingly. <Satan himself! But if you want my claws, sir, you shall have them.>

<I, too, will aid you,> Polly says, <though I confess I am unsure what we can do against such an enemy.>

<This time there will be four of us,> Black Tom says. <Four cats! The devil won't know what hit him.>

<This is the wrong strategy,> says the Nighthunter Moppet, and her voice has the ring of a blade unsheathed.

All kittenness has fallen away from Moppet. What sits before the milk bowl is the ruthless killer of the courtyard, the assassin whose title *nighthunter* is whispered in terror among the mice and birds of Bethnal Green. It is rumored that the Moppet's great-grandmother was a demon of the lower realms, which might perhaps explain the peculiar keenness of her green-glass eyes, and her talent for death-dealing. Indeed, as Jeoffry watches, the Moppet's tiny shadow seems to grow and split into seven pieces, each of which is shaped like a monstrous cat with seven tails. The shadow cats' tails lash and lash as the Nighthunter Moppet broods on Satan.

<It is true that as cats we are descended from the Angel Tiger, who killed the Ichneumon-rat of Egypt,> says the Moppet. Her shadows twist into the shapes of rats and angels as she speaks. **<We are warriors of God, and as such, we can blood Satan. But we cannot kill him, for he has another fate decreed.>**

The Nighthunter Moppet sighs at the thought of a lost kill, and drops her gaze to the ground. The brown beetle is still there, trotting over the cobblestones. She begins to follow it with her nose.

<Moppet!> Polly says sternly. <You were telling us how we should fight the devil!>
<Oh sorry, sorry,> the Moppet says. With great effort she tears her gaze away from the beetle. Instantly her seven shadows are back, larger than before, raising their claws to the heavens.

<To win this fight we must think carefully of what we mean to win,> says the Nighthunter Moppet. The pupils have disappeared from her eyes, which blaze green fire. **<Is it Satan's death? No. His humiliation? Again, no.>**

<Speak for yourself,> Black Tom says. <He will run from my claws!>

The kitten's shadows turn and look at Black Tom with disapproval. When she next speaks, their voices join hers. They sound like the buzzing of a thousand flies.

<It is neither of those things!> cry the army of Moppets. **<Think! What is it the devil hopes to achieve?>**

<The destruction of the world,> says Polly.

<A poem about his greatness,> says Black Tom.

<The poet's soul,> says Jeoffry.

<Exactly,> snarl the Moppets. **<And those three things are also one thing. If you steal it from him, good cat Jeoffry, then you will have beaten the devil.>** With that her shadows shrink back into a normal, kitten-shaped shadow, and the pupils return to her green eyes.

<But what do I steal?> Jeoffry asks desperately.

The Moppet looks at him blankly. <What?> she says. <Are we stealing something?>

<I think the Nighthunter Moppet has told us all she can, Jeoffry,> Polly says.

<But it is not enough,> Jeoffry says. Thinking is harder than fighting, and his head hurts. Still. He squeezes his eyes tightly, and thinks over all that has happened. The poet. The devil. The Poem of Poems.

<I think I know what I must do,> he says. <But to do it I must sneak past the devil, and his eyes are keen.>

<We shall help you,> says Black Tom.

<We shall fight him,> says Polly.

The light of spirit fire flickers in the Nighthunter's eyes. Some of her shadows peer out from behind her body.

<And you,> she intones, ***<shall creep.>***

That night the devil is in a good mood. He whistles as he walks between the stars, cracking the tip of his cane on the pathway. From time to time, this dislodges a young star, who falls screaming.

"Good evening, good fellow," he says to the sleeping night watchman as he enters the asylum. "And to you,

Bently," he says as he passes a cell containing a murderer. The man shrieks and scuttles away. Finally the devil arrives at the poet's cell. "And how do you do, Mr. Smart? Do you have my poem?"

The poet crouches, terrified, in the corner of his cell. No, no—please, Jesus, no, he moans. But there is a sheet of paper quivering in his hand.

"Excellent," the devil says. "Come now, hand it over. You'll feel much better once you do."

The poet is jerked upright, like an ill-strung marionette. The hand that clasps the paper swings away from his body. But as the devil reaches to claim it, there is a yowl from behind him.

<Stand and deliver, you d——d mangy w———n!> It is Black Tom, his tail bristling like a brush.

At his side, Polly narrows her eyes. <Sir, you must step away from that poet!>

"What's this?" The devil puts his hands on his hips and regards the growling cats. "More cats come to terrorize my stockings?"

<We'll have more than your stockings, sir,> says Polly.

<D—n your eyes, I'll have your hide, you ——— ——— ————— —— ——!!!!>

"Such language!" says the devil. Even Polly looks shocked.

"Well, sir," Satan says, "I'll not be called a ——— by anyone, let alone by a flea-bitten alley cat. Lay on, sir!" And the devil is a cat again, and an angel, and an angry critic raising his walking stick as a club. Even as the devil's walking stick swings down in a slow, glittering arc of hellfire, even as the devil aims to crack the top of Black Tom's dancing, prancing skull, a bloodcurdling cry rings out from above.

<I AM THE NIGHTHUNTER MOPPET!>

Perched on a dusty sconce above the devil's head is a rabid, knife-jawed, fire-eyed kitten with seven hungry shadows. And as the devil looks up agape, she springs, her wicked claws catching the light, right on top of the devil's powdered wig.

Hellfire! Chaos! The two other cats rush the devil's legs, clawing at his face. He bites and clobbers them, his wings and fists swinging. The walls of the asylum throb with the impact of the battle. The poet, crumpled on the floor, twitches and writhes. In every cell, the lunatics begin to howl.

Jeoffry lays back his ears and continues to *creep,* as the Moppet showed him. <**We are descended from angels,**> she had said, <**and as such we can move into the spaces between the world-we-see and the world-that-is.**>

That is where Jeoffry is now, slinking past the devil on a slanted path of broken stardust, in a fold of space where the keen-eyed Adversary would not think to look. Creeping is hard to do, not just because Jeoffry has to squeeze every ounce of his catness into this cosmic folding, but also because there is a brawl happening at his back that he would dearly love to join.

Since when does Jeoffry, the most glorious warrior of catdom, slink away from a fight? whispers a voice inside him. *Since when is Jeoffry a coward? Will he let Black Tom get the glory of defeating the devil?*

But Jeoffry shuts his ear to this voice. He has learned that there is more than one kind of devil, and that the one inside your head, that speaks with the voice of your own heart, is far more dangerous than the velvet coat–wearing, poetry-loving variety.

Indeed, the fiend is having a harder time against three cats than he did against one. One of his shadows has turned into a dragon and is fighting Black Tom; Satan's powdered wig has animated itself and is tackling Polly across the hallway. But in the center of the poet's cell, in a storm of lightning and hellfire, whirl Satan and the Nighthunter Moppet, splattered with each other's blood. The Moppet has only five shadows now, and one of her green eyes is closed, but her snarl still gleams prettily amid the flames of darkness visible.

"Stand down, you vile kitten!"

<I AM! NIGHTHUNTER! MOPPET!> the kitten screams back. As battle cries go, it is unoriginal, but gets the central point across, Jeoffry thinks as he slinks ever closer to the gibbering poet. The ghosts of the stars Satan has lately killed whisper encouragement as he creeps forward through cosmic space, inch by careful inch.

"You cannot win," Satan says. At that, he seems to collect himself. The various pieces of the devil reassemble in a column of fire at the center of the room (with the exception of the powdered wig, which Polly has pinned down on the staircase). "This poet is mine. And if you oppose me further, you will die."

<We shall die, then,> Polly says, a tuft of whitened hair hanging from her teeth. Behind her, the powdered wig, its curls in disarray, scrunches down the staircase to freedom.

<F—k you,> says Black Tom.

On the floor, the crumpled shape of a small black kitten staggers to its feet. <Nighthunter.> It says. <Moppet.>

"Very well," the dragon/cat/critic says, and opens its jaws.

And Jeoffry stops *creeping*. He springs.

Fire and flood! Wonder and horror! Jeoffry has snatched the sheet of paper from the poet's trembling hand and swallowed it whole! Snap snap! The paper on the table is eaten too! Snap! And the crumpled drafts on the floor! Jeoffry is a whirlwind of gluttony! As a last measure, he knocks over the ink bottle and laps it up. Glug glug! Take that, Satan!

The devil stands in the center of the cell, cats dangling from his arms. The look on his face is similar to the one he wore at his defeat in the Battle of Heaven, and is only marginally happier than the one he wore on his arrival in Hell.

Normally, when Satan wears that expression, it is a sign he is about to begin speechifying. But for once, all his words are gone. They are sitting inside a belching ginger cat, who blinks at the devil and licks his lips.

"Oh hell, cat," says the devil, letting the half-throttled felines fall to the floor. "What have you done?"

Jeoffry grins at him. He can feel a warm glow inside him that is the poet's soul, being safely digested. His soul was in the poem, the poet said, and now Jeoffry has eaten it up. The devil cannot have it now.

"No!" the devil shrieks. He rages. He stomps his foot. He puts his hands to his head and tears himself in half, and the separate halves of him explode in angry fireworks.

Then, perhaps thinking better of his dignity, the devil re-manifests and straightens his waistcoat. He glares at Jeoffry. "You," he says, "have scarred literature forever. You stupid cat."

With that, the devil turns on his heel and leaves.

The poet in the corner staggers forward. Thank Jesus! he cries. Jeoffry, you have done it!

<And me,> says Black Tom.

<All of us did it,> says Polly.

<The devil forgot his wig,> the Nighthunter Moppet says. Her one good eye narrows.

<Thank you, thank you, my friends,> Jeoffry says. <I am forever obliged for your help in this.> And then he winds himself around the poet and purrs.

That is the story of how the devil came to the madhouse, and was defeated (though not in battle) by the great Jeoffry. There are other stories I could tell, of the sea battles of Black Tom, of Polly's foray into opera, and of the Nighthunter Moppet's epic hunt for Satan's wig, which left a trail of mischief and misery across London for years.

But instead I will end with poetry.

FOR HE CAN CREEP

For I will consider my Cat Jeoffry.

For he is the servant of the Living God duly and daily serving him.

....

For he keeps the Lord's watch in the night against the Adversary.

For he counteracts the powers of Darkness by his electrical skin and glaring eyes.

For he counteracts the Devil, who is death, by brisking about the life.

....

For he can creep.

—Christopher Smart
St. Luke's Hospital for Lunatics,
c. 1763

SPIDER ROSE

Bruce Sterling

Nothing was what Spider Rose felt, or almost nothing. There had been some feelings there, a nexus of clotted two-hundred-year-old emotions, and she had mashed it with a cranial injection. Now what was left of her feelings was like what is left of a roach when a hammer strikes it.

Spider Rose knew about roaches; they were the only native animal life in the orbiting Mechanist colonies. They had plagued spacecraft from the beginning, too tough, prolific, and adaptable to kill. Of necessity, the Mechanists had used genetic techniques stolen from their rivals the Shapers to turn the roaches into colorful pets. One of Spider Rose's special favorites was a roach a foot long and covered with red and yellow pigment squiggles against shiny black chitin. It was clinging to her head. It drank sweat from her perfect brow, and she knew nothing, for she was elsewhere, watching for visitors.

She watched through eight telescopes, their images collated and fed into her brain through a nerve-crystal junction at the base of her skull. She had eight eyes now, like her symbol, the spider. Her ears were the weak steady pulse of radar, listening, listening for the weird distortion that would signal the presence of an Investor ship.

Rose was clever. She might have been insane, but her monitoring techniques established the chemical basis of sanity and maintained it artificially. Spider Rose accepted this as normal.

And it was normal; not for human beings, but for a two-hundred-year-old Mechanist, living in a spinning web of a habitat orbiting Uranus, her body seething with youth hormones, her wise old-young face like something pulled fresh from a plaster mold, her long white hair a rippling display of implanted fiber-optic threads with tiny beads of light oozing like microscopic gems from their slant-cut tips … She was old, but she didn't think about that. And she was lonely, but she had crushed those feelings with drugs. And she had something that the Investors wanted, something that those reptilian alien traders would give their eye-fangs to possess.

Trapped in her polycarbon spiderweb, the wide-stretched cargo net that had given her her name, she had a jewel the size of a bus.

And so she watched, brain-linked to her instruments, tireless, not particularly interested but certainly not bored. Boredom was dangerous. It led to unrest, and unrest could be fatal in a space habitat, where malice or even plain carelessness could kill. The proper survival behavior was this: to crouch in the center of the mental web, clean euclidean web-lines of rationality radiating out in all directions, hooked legs alert for the slightest tremble of troubling emotion. And when she sensed that feeling tangling the lines, she rushed there, gauged it, shrouded it neatly, and pierced it cleanly and lingeringly with a spiderfang hypodermic …

There it was. Her octuple eyes gazed a quarter of a million miles into space and spotted the star-rippling warp of an Investor ship. The Investor ships had no conventional engines, and radiated no detectable energies; the secret of their star drive was closely guarded. All that any of the factions (still loosely called "humanity" for lack of a better term) knew for sure about the Investor drive was that it sent long parabolic streamers of distortion from the sterns of ships, causing a rippling effect against the background of stars.

Spider Rose came partially out of her static observation mode and felt herself in her body once more. The computer signals were muted now, overlaid behind her normal vision like a reflection of her own face on a glass window as she gazed through it. Touching a keyboard, she pinpointed the Investor ship with a communications laser and sent it a pulse of data: a business offer. (Radio was too chancy; it might attract Shaper pirates, and she had had to kill three of them already.)

She knew she had been heard and understood when she saw the Investor ship perform a dead stop and an angled acceleration that broke every known law of orbital dynamics. While she waited, Spider Rose loaded an Investor translator program. It was fifty years old, but the Investors were a persistent lot, not so much conservative as just uninterested in change.

When it came too close to her station for star-drive maneuvers, the Investor ship unfurled a decorated solar sail with a puff of gas. The sail was big enough to gift-wrap a small moon and thinner than a two-hundred-year-old memory. Despite its fantastic thinness, there were molecule-thin murals worked onto it: titanic scenes of Investor argosies where wily Investors had defrauded pebbly bipeds and gullible heavy-planet gasbags swollen with wealth and hydrogen. The great jewel-laden queens of the Investor race, surrounded by adoring male harems, flaunted their gaudy sophistication above miles-high narratives of Investor hieroglyphs, placed on a musical grid to indicate the proper pitch and intonation of their half-sung language.

There was a burst of static on the screen before her and an Investor face appeared. Spider Rose pulled the plug from her neck. She studied the face: its great glassy eyes half-shrouded behind nictitating membranes, rainbow frill behind pinhole-sized ears, bumpy skin, reptile grin with peg-sized teeth. It made noises: "Ship's ensign here," her computer translated. "Lydia Martinez?"

"Yes," Spider Rose said, not bothering to explain that her name had changed. She had had many names.

“We had profitable dealings with your husband in the past,” the Investor said with interest. “How does he fare these days?”

“He died thirty years ago,” Spider Rose said. She had mashed the grief. “Shaper assassins killed him.”

The Investor officer flickered his frill. He was not embarrassed. Embarrassment was not an emotion native to Investors. “Bad for business,” he opined. “Where is this jewel you mentioned?”

“Prepare for incoming data,” said Spider Rose, touching her keyboard. She watched the screen as her carefully prepared sales spiel unrolled itself, its communication beam shielded to avoid enemy ears.

It had been the find of a lifetime. It had started existence as part of a glacierlike ice moon of the protoplanet Uranus, shattering, melting, and recrystallizing in the primeval eons of relentless bombardment. It had cracked at least four different times, and each time mineral flows had been forced within its fracture zones under tremendous pressure: carbon, manganese silicate, beryllium, aluminum oxide. When the moon was finally broken up into the famous Ring complex, the massive ice chunk had floated for eons, awash in shock waves of hard radiation, accumulating and losing charge in the bizarre electromagnetic flickerings typical of all Ring formations.

And then one crucial moment some millions of years ago it had been ground-zero for a titanic lightning flash, one of those soundless invisible gouts of electric energy, dissipating charges built up over whole decades. Most of the ice-chunk’s outer envelope had flashed off at once as a plasma. The rest was … changed. Mineral occlusions were now strings and veins of beryl, shading here and there into lumps of raw emerald big as Investors’ heads, crisscrossed with nets of red corundum and purple garnet. There were lumps of fused diamond, weirdly colored blazing diamond that came only from the strange quantum states of metallic carbon. Even the ice itself had changed into something rich and unique and therefore by definition precious.

"You intrigue us," the Investor said. For them, this was profound enthusiasm. Spider Rose smiled. The ensign continued: "This is an unusual commodity and its value is hard to establish. We offer you a quarter of a million gigawatts."

Spider Rose said, "I have the energy I need to run my station and defend myself. Its generous, but I could never store that much."

"We will also give you a stabilized plasma lattice for storage." This unexpected and fabulous generosity was meant to overwhelm her. The construction of plasma lattices was far beyond human technology, and to own one would be a ten years' wonder. It was the last thing she wanted. "Not interested," she said.

The Investor lifted his frill. "Not interested in the basic currency of galactic trade?"

"Not when I can spend it only with you."

"Trade with young races is a thankless lot," the Investor observed. "I suppose you want information, then. You young races always want to trade in technology. We have some Shaper techniques for trade within their faction—are you interested in those?"

"Industrial espionage?" Spider Rose said. "You should have tried me eighty years ago. No, I know you Investors too well. You would only sell Mechanist techniques to them to maintain the balance of power."

"We like a competitive market," the Investor admitted. "It helps us avoid painful monopoly situations like the one we face now, dealing with you."

"I don't want power of any kind. Status means nothing to me. Show me something new."

"No status? What will your fellows think?"

"I live alone."

The Investor hid his eyes behind nictitating membranes. "Crushed your gregarious instincts? An ominous development. Well, I will take a new tack. Will you consider weaponry? If you will agree to various conditions regarding their use, we can give you unique and powerful armaments."

"I manage already."

"You could use our political skills. We can strongly influence the major Shaper groups and protect you from them by treaty. It would take ten or twenty years, but it could be done."

"It's up to them to be afraid of me," Spider Rose said, "not vice versa."

"A new habitat, then." The Investor was patient. "You can live within solid gold."

"I like what I have."

"We have some artifacts that might amuse you," the Investor said. "Prepare for incoming data."

Spider Rose spent eight hours examining the various wares. There was no hurry. She was too old for impatience, and the Investors lived to bargain.

She was offered colorful algae cultures that produced oxygen and alien perfumes. There were metafoil structures of collapsed atoms for radiation shielding and defense. Rare techniques that transmuted nerve fibers to crystal. A smooth black wand that made iron so malleable that you could mold it with your hands and set it in shape. A small luxury submarine for the exploration of ammonia and methane seas, made of transparent metallic glass. Self-replicating globes of patterned silica that, as they grew, played out a game simulating the birth, growth, and decline of an alien culture. A land-sea-and-aircraft so tiny that you buttoned it on like a suit. "I don't care for planets," Spider Rose said. "I don't like gravity wells."

"Under certain circumstances we could make a gravity generator available," the Investor said. "It would have to be tamper-proof, like the wand and the weapons, and loaned rather than sold outright. We must avoid the escape of such a technology."

She shrugged. "Our own technologies have shattered us. We can't assimilate what we already have. I see no reason to burden myself with more."

"This is all we can offer you that's not on the interdicted list," he said. "This ship in particular has a great many items suitable only for races that live at very low temperature and very high pressure. And we have items that you would probably enjoy a great deal, but they would kill you. Or your whole species. The literature of the [untranslatable], for instance."

"I can read the literature of Earth if I want an alien viewpoint," she said.

"[Untranslatable] is not really a literature," the Investor said benignly. "It's really a kind of virus."

A roach flew onto her shoulder. "Pets!" he said. "Pets! You enjoy them?"

"They are my solace," she said, letting it nibble the cuticle of her thumb.

"I should have thought," he said. "Give me twelve hours."

She went to sleep. After she woke, she studied the alien craft through her telescope while she waited. All Investor ships were covered with fantastic designs in hammered metal: animal heads, metal mosaics, scenes and inscriptions in deep relief, as well as cargo bays and instruments. But experts had pointed out that the basic shape beneath the ornamentation was always the same: a simple octahedron with six long rectangular sides. The Investors had gone to some pains to disguise this fact; and the current theory held that the ships had been bought, found, or stolen from a more advanced race. Certainly the Investors, with their whimsical attitude toward science and technology, seemed incapable of building them themselves.

The ensign reopened contact. His nictitating membranes looked whiter than usual. He held up a small winged reptilian being with a long spiny crest the color of an Investor's frill. "This is our Commander's mascot, called 'Little Nose for Profits.' Beloved by us all! It costs us a pang to part from him. We had to choose between losing face in this business deal or losing his company." He toyed with it. It grasped his thick digits with little scaly hands.

"He's ... cute," she said, finding a half-forgotten word from her childhood and pronouncing it with a grimace of distaste. "But I'm not going to trade my find for some carnivorous lizardkin."

"And think of us!" the Investor lamented. "Condemning our little Nose to an alien lair swarming with bacteria and giant vermin ... However, this can't be helped. Here's our proposal. You take our mascot for seven hundred plus or minus five of your days. We will return here on our way out of your system. You can choose then between owning him or keeping your prize. In the meantime you must promise not to sell the jewel or inform anyone else of its existence."

"You mean that you will leave me your pet as a kind of earnest money on the transaction."

The Investor covered his eyes with the nictitating membranes and squeezed his pebbly lids half-shut. It was a sign of acute distress. "He is a hostage to your cruel indecision, Lydia Martinez. Frankly we doubt that we can find anything in this system that can satisfy you better than our mascot can. Except perhaps some novel mode of suicide."

Spider Rose was surprised. She had never seen an Investor become so emotionally involved. Generally they seemed to take a detached view of life, even showing on occasion behavior patterns that resembled a sense of humor.

She was enjoying herself. She was past the point when any of the Investor's normal commodities could have tempted her. In essence, she was trading her jewel for an interior mind-state: not an emotion, because she mashed those, but for a paler and cleaner feeling: interestedness. She wanted to be interested, to find something to occupy herself besides dead stones and space. And this looked intriguing.

"All right," she said. "I agree. Seven hundred plus or minus five days. And I keep silence." She smiled. She hadn't spoken to another human in five years and was not about to start.

"Take good care of our Little Nose for Profits," the Investor said, half pleading, half warning, accenting those nuances so that her computer would be sure to pick them up. "We will still want him, even if, through some utter corrosion of the spirit, you do not. He is valuable and rare. We will send you instructions on his care and feeding. Prepare for incoming data."

They fired the creature's cargo capsule into the tight-stretched polycarbon web of her spider habitat. The web was built on a framework of eight spokes, and these spokes were pulled taut by centrifugal force from the wheeling rotation of eight teardrop-shaped capsules. At the impact of the cargo shot, the web bowed gracefully and the eight massive metal teardrops were pulled closer to the web's center in short, graceful free-fall arcs. Wan sunlight glittered along the web as it expanded in recoil, its rotation slowed a little by the energy it had spent in absorbing the inertia. It was a cheap and effective docking technique, for a rate of spin was much easier to manage than complex maneuvering.

Hook-legged industrial robots ran quickly along the polycarbon fibers and seized the mascot's capsule with clamps and magnetic palps. Spider Rose ran the lead robot herself, feeling and seeing through its grips and cameras. The robots hustled the cargo craft to an airlock, dislodged its contents, and attached a small parasitic rocket to boost it back to the Investor mother ship. After the small rocket had returned and the Investor ship had left, the robots trooped back to their teardrop garages and shut themselves off, waiting for the next tremor of the web.

Spider Rose disconnected herself and opened the airlock. The mascot flew into the room. It had seemed tiny compared to the Investor ensign, but the Investors were huge. The mascot was as tall as her knee. Wheezing musically on the unfamiliar air, it flew around the room, ducking and darting unevenly.

A roach launched itself from the wall and flew with a great clatter of wings. The mascot hit the deck with a squawk of terror and lay there, comically feeling its spindly arms and legs for damage. It half-closed its rough eyelids. Like the eyes of an Investor baby, Spider Rose thought suddenly, though she had never seen a young Investor and doubted if anyone human ever had. She had a dim memory of something she had heard a long time before—something about pets and babies, their large heads, their large eyes, their softness, their dependence. She remembered scoffing at the idea that the sloppy dependence of, say, a "dog" or "cat" could rival the clean economy and efficiency of a roach.

The Investor mascot had recovered its composure and was crouching bent-kneed on the algae carpet, warbling to itself. There was a sort of sly grin on its miniature dragon face. Its half-slitted eyes were alert and its matchstick ribs moved up and down with each breath. Its pupils were huge. Spider Rose imagined that it must find the light very dim. The lights in Investor ships were like searing blue arc-lamps, drenched in ultraviolet.

"We have to find a new name for you," Spider Rose said. "I don't speak Investor, so I can't use the name they gave you."

The mascot fixed her with a friendly stare, and it arched little half-transparent flaps over its pinhole ears. Real Investors had no such flaps, and she was charmed at this further deviation from the norm. Actually, except for the wings, it looked altogether too much like a tiny Investor. The effect was creepy.

"I'll call you Fuzzy," she said. It had no hair. It was a private joke, but all her jokes were private.

The mascot bounced across the floor. The false centrifugal gravity was lighter here, too, than the 1.3 g's that the massive Investors used. It embraced her bare leg and licked her kneecap with a rough sandpaper tongue. She laughed, more than a little alarmed, but she knew the Investors were strictly nonaggressive. A pet of theirs would not be dangerous.

It made eager chirping sounds and climbed onto her head, clutching handfuls of glittering optic fibers. She sat at her data console and called up the care and feeding instructions.

Clearly the Investors had not expected to trade their pet, because the instructions were almost indecipherable. They had the air of a second- or third-hand translation from some even more profoundly alien language. However, true to Investor tradition, the blandly pragmatic aspects had been emphasized.

Spider Rose relaxed. Apparently the mascots would eat almost anything, though they preferred dextrorotatory proteins and required certain easily acquirable trace minerals. They were extremely resistant to toxins and had no native intestinal bacteria. (Neither did the Investors themselves, and they regarded races who did as savages.)

She looked for its respiratory requirements as the mascot leapt from her head and capered across the control board, almost aborting the program. She shooed it off, hunting for something she could comprehend amid dense clusters of alien graphs and garbled technical material. Suddenly she recognized something from her old days in technical espionage: a genetics chart.

She frowned. It seemed she had run past the relevant sections and on to another treatise entirely. She advanced the data slightly and discovered a three-dimensional illustration of some kind of fantastically complex genetic construct, with long helical chains of alien genes marked out in improbable colors. The gene chains were wrapped around long spires or spicules that emerged radially from a dense central knot. Further chains of tightly wound helices connected spire to spire. Apparently these chains activated different sections of genetic material from their junctions on the spires, for she could see ghost chains of slave proteins peeling off from some of the activated genes.

Spider Rose smiled. No doubt a skilled Shaper geneticist could profit spectacularly from these plans. It amused her to think that they never would. Obviously this was some kind of alien industrial genetic complex, for there was more genetic hardware there than any actual living animal could ever possibly need.

She knew that the Investors themselves never tampered with genetics. She wondered which of the nineteen known intelligent races had originated this thing. It might even have come from outside the Investors' economic realm, or it might be a relic from one of the extinct races.

She wondered if she ought to erase the data. If she died, it might fall into the wrong hands. As she thought of her death, the first creeping shades of a profound depression disturbed her. She allowed the sensation to build for a moment while she thought. The Investors had been careless to leave her with this information; or perhaps they underestimated the genetic abilities of the smooth and charismatic Shapers with their spectacularly boosted IQs.

There was a wobbling feeling inside her head. For a dizzying moment the chemically repressed emotions gushed forth with all their pent-up force. She felt an agonized envy for the Investors, for the dumb arrogance and confidence that allowed them to cruise the stars screwing their purported inferiors. She wanted to be with them. She wanted to get aboard a magic ship and feel alien sunlight burn her skin in some place light-years from human weakness. She wanted to scream and feel like a little girl had screamed and felt one hundred and ninety-three years ago on a roller coaster in Los Angeles, screaming in total pure intensity of feeling, in swept-away sensation like she had felt in the arms of her husband, her man dead now thirty years. Dead … Thirty years …

Her hands trembling, she opened a drawer beneath the control board. She smelled the faint medicinal reek of ozone from the sterilizer. Blindly she pushed her glittering hair from the plastic duct into her skull, pressed the injector against it, inhaled once, closed her eyes, inhaled twice, pulled the hypo away. Her eyes glazed over as she refilled the hypo and slipped it back into its velcro holster in the drawer.

She held the bottle and looked at it blankly. There was still plenty left. She would not have to synthesize more for months. Her brain felt like someone had stepped on it. It was always like this right after a mash. She shut off the Investor data and filed it absently in an obscure corner of computer memory. From its stand on the laser-corn interface the mascot sang briefly and groomed its wing.

Soon she was herself again. She smiled. These sudden attacks were something she took for granted. She took an oral tranquilizer to stop the trembling of her hands and antacid for the stress on her stomach.

Then she played with the mascot until it grew tired and went to sleep. For four days she fed it carefully, being especially careful not to overfeed it, for like its models the Investors, it was a greedy little creature and she was afraid it would hurt itself. Even despite its rough skin and cold-bloodedness she was growing fond of it. When it grew tired of begging for food, it would play with string for hours or sit on her head watching the screen as she monitored the mining robots she had out in the Rings.

On the fifth day she found on awakening that it had killed and eaten her four largest and fattest roaches. Filled with a righteous anger she did nothing to blunt, she hunted for it throughout the capsule.

She did not find it. Instead, after hours of search, she found a mascot-sized cocoon wedged under the toilet.

♥ ✖ ■

It had gone into some sort of hibernation. She forgave it for eating the roaches. They were easy to replace, anyway, and rivals for her affections. In a way it was flattering. But the sharp pang of worry she felt overrode that. She examined the cocoon closely. It was made of overlapping sheets of some brittle translucent substance—dried mucus?—that she could chip easily with her fingernail. The cocoon was not perfectly rounded; there were small vague lumps that might have been its knees and elbows. She took another injection.

The week it spent in hibernation was a period of acute anxiety for her. She pored over the Investor tapes, but they were far too cryptic for her limited expertise. At least she knew it was not dead, for the cocoon was warm to the touch and the lumps within it sometimes stirred.

She was asleep when it began to break free of the cocoon. She had set up monitors to warn her, however, and she rushed to it at the first alarm.

The cocoon was splitting. A rent appeared in the brittle overlapping sheets, and a warm animal reek seeped out into the recycled air.

Then a paw emerged: a tiny five-fingered paw covered in glittering fur. A second paw poked through, and the two paws gripped the edges of the rent and ripped the cocoon away. It stepped out into the light, kicking the husk aside with a little human shuffle, and it grinned.

It looked like a little ape, small and soft and glittering. There were tiny human teeth behind the human lips of its grin. It had small soft baby's feet on the ends of its round springy legs, and it had lost its wings. Its eyes were the color of her eyes. The smooth mammalian skin of its round little face had the faint rosy flush of perfect health.

It jumped into the air, and she saw the pink of its tongue as it babbled aloud in human syllables.

It skipped over and embraced her leg. She was frightened, amazed, and profoundly relieved. She petted the soft perfect glittering fur on its hard little nugget of a head.

"Fuzzy," she said. "I'm glad. I'm very glad."

"Wa wa wa," it said, mimicking her intonation in its piping child's voice. Then it skipped back to its cocoon and began to eat it by the double handful, grinning.

She understood now why the Investors had been so reluctant to offer their mascot. It was a trade item of fantastic value. It was a genetic artifact, able to judge the emotional wants and needs of an alien species and adapt itself to them in a matter of days.

She began to wonder why the Investors had given it away at all; if they fully understood the capabilities of their pet. Certainly she doubted that they had understood the complex data that had come with it. Very likely, they had acquired the mascot from other Investors, in its reptilian form. It was even possible (the thought chilled her) that it might be older than the entire Investor race.

She stared at it: at its clear, guileless, trusting eyes. It gripped her fingers with small warm sinewy hands. Unable to resist, she hugged it to her, and it babbled with pleasure. Yes, it could easily have lived for hundreds or thousands of years, spreading its love (or equivalent emotions) among dozens of differing species.

And who would harm it? Even the most depraved and hardened of her own species had secret weaknesses. She remembered stories of guards in concentration camps who butchered men and women without a qualm, but meticulously fed hungry birds in the winter. Fear bred fear and hatred, but how could anyone feel fear or hatred toward this creature, or resist its brilliant powers?

It was not intelligent; it didn't need intelligence. It was sexless as well. An ability to breed would have ruined its value as a trade item. Besides, she doubted that anything so complex could have grown in a womb. Its genes would have to be built, spicule by spicule, in some unimaginable lab.

Days and weeks reeled by. Its ability to sense her moods was little short of miraculous. When she needed it, it was always there, and when she didn't it vanished. Sometimes she would hear it chattering to itself as it capered in strange acrobatics or chased and ate roaches. It was never mischievous, and on the odd occasions where it spilled food or upset something, it would unobtrusively clean up after itself. It dropped its small inoffensive fecal pellets into the same recycler she used.

These were the only signs it showed of patterns of thought that were more than animal. Once, and only once, it had mimicked her, repeating a sentence letter-perfect. She had been shocked, and it had sensed her reaction immediately. It never tried to parrot her again.

They slept in the same bed. Sometimes while she slept she would feel its warm nose snuffling lightly along the surface of her skin, as if it could smell her suppressed moods and feelings through the pores. Sometimes it would rub or press with its small firm hands against her neck or spine, and there was always a tightened muscle there that relaxed in gratitude. She never allowed this in the day, but at night, when her discipline was half-dissolved in sleep, there was a conspiracy between them.

The Investors had been gone over six hundred days. She laughed when she thought of the bargain she was getting.

The sound of her own laughter no longer startled her. She had even cut back on her dosages of suppressants and inhibitors. Her pet seemed so much happier when she was happy, and when it was at hand her ancient sadnesses seemed easier to bear. One by one she began to face old pains and traumas, holding her pet close and shedding healing tears into its glittering fur. One by one it licked her tears, tasting the emotional chemicals they contained, smelling her breath and skin, holding her as she was racked with sobbing. There were so many memories. She felt old, horribly old, but at the same time she felt a new sense of wholeness that allowed her to bear it. She had done things in the past—cruel things—and she had never put up with the inconvenience of guilt. She had mashed it instead.

Now for the first time in decades she felt the vague reawakening of a sense of purpose. She wanted to see people again—dozens of people, hundreds of people, all of whom would admire her, protect her, find her precious, whom she could care for, who would keep her safer than she was with only one companion …

Her web station entered the most dangerous part of its orbit, where it crossed the plane of the Rings. Here she was busiest, accepting the drifting chunks of raw materials-ice, carbonaceous chondrites, metal ores—that her telepuppet mining robots had discovered and sent her way. There were killers in these Rings: rapacious pirates, paranoid settlers anxious to lash out.

In her normal orbit, far off the plane of the ecliptic, she was safe. But here there were orders to be broadcasted, energies to be spent, the telltale traces of powerful mass drivers hooked to the captive asteroids she claimed and mined. It was an unavoidable risk. Even the best-designed habitat was not a completely closed system, and hers was big, and old.

They found her.

Three ships. She tried bluffing them off at first, sending them a standard interdiction warning routed through a telepuppet beacon. They found the beacon and destroyed it, but that gave her their location and some blurry data through the beacon's limited sensors.

Three sleek ships, iridescent capsules half-metal, half-organic, with long ribbed insect-tinted sun-wings thinner than the scum of oil on water. Shaper spacecraft, knobbed with the geodesies of sensors, the spines of magnetic and optical weapons systems, long cargo manipulators folded like the arms of mantises.

She sat hooked into her own sensors, studying them,

taking in a steady trickle of data: range estimation, target probabilities, weapons status. Radar was too risky; she sighted them optically. This was fine for lasers, but her lasers were not her best weapons. She might get one, but the others would be on her. It was better that she stay quiet while they prowled the Rings and she slid silently off the ecliptic.

But they had found her. She saw them fold their sails and activate their ion engines.

They were sending radio. She entered it on screen, not wanting the distraction filling her head. A Shaper's face appeared, one of the Oriental-based gene lines, smooth raven hair held back with jeweled pins, slim black eyebrows arched over dark eyes with the epicanthic fold, pale lips slightly curved in a charismatic smile. A smooth, clean actor's face with the glittering ageless eyes of a fanatic. "Jade Prime," she said.

"Colonel-Doctor Jade Prime," the Shaper said, fingering a golden insignia of rank in the collar of his black military tunic. "Still calling yourself 'Spider Rose' these days, Lydia? Or have you wiped that out of your brain?"

"Why are you a soldier instead of a corpse?"

"Times change, Spider. The bright young lights get snuffed out, by your old friends, and those of us with long-range plans are left to settle old debts. You remember old debts, Spider?"

"You think you're going to survive this meeting, don't you, Prime?" She felt the muscles of her face knotting with a ferocious hatred she had no time to kill. "Three ships manned with your own clones. How long have you holed up in that rock of yours, like a maggot in an apple? Cloning and cloning. When was the last time a woman let you touch her?"

His eternal smile twisted into a leer with bright teeth behind it. "It's no use, Spider. You've already killed thirty-seven of me, and I just keep coming back, don't I? You pathetic old bitch, what the hell is a maggot, anyway? Something like that mutant on your shoulder?"

She hadn't even known the pet was there, and her heart was stabbed with fear for it. "You've come too close!"

"Fire, then! Shoot me, you germy old cretin! Fire!"

"You're not him!" she said suddenly. "You're not First Jade! Hah! He's dead, isn't he?"

The clone's face twisted with rage. Lasers flared, and three of her habitats melted into slag and clouds of metallic plasma. A last searing pulse of intolerable brightness flashed in her brain from three melting telescopes.

She cut loose with a chugging volley of magnetically accelerated iron slugs. At four hundred miles per second they riddled the first ship and left it gushing air and brittle clouds of freezing water.

Two ships fired. They used weapons she had never seen before, and they crushed two habitats like a pair of giant fists. The web lurched with the impact, its equilibrium gone. She knew instantly which weapons systems were left, and she returned fire with metal-jacketed pellets of ammonia ice. They punched through the semiorganic sides of a second Shaper craft. The tiny holes sealed instantly, but the crew was finished; the ammonia vaporized inside, releasing instantly lethal nerve toxins.

The last ship had one chance in three to get her command center. Two hundred years of luck ran out for Spider Rose. Static stung her hands from the controls. Every light in the habitat went out, and her computer underwent a total crash. She screamed and waited for death.

Death did not come.

Her mouth gushed with the bile of nausea. She opened the drawer in the darkness and filled her brain with liquid tranquillity. Breathing hard, she sat back in her console chair, her panic mashed. "Electromagnetic pulse," she said. "Stripped everything I had."

The pet warbled a few syllables. "He would have finished us by now if he could," she told her pet. "The defenses must have come through from the other habitats when the mainframe crashed."

She felt a thump as the pet jumped into her lap, shivering with terror. She hugged it absently, rubbing its slender neck. "Let's see," she said into the darkness. "The ice toxins are down, I had them overridden from here." She pulled the useless plug from her neck and plucked her robe away from her damp ribs. "It was the spray, then. A nice, thick cloud of hot ionized metallic copper. Blew every sensor he had. He's riding blind in a metallic coffin. Just like us."

She laughed. "Except old Rose has a trick left, baby. The Investors. They'll be looking for me. There's nobody left to look for him. And I still have my rock."

She sat silently, and her artificial calmness allowed her to think the unthinkable. The pet stirred uneasily, sniffing at her skin. It had calmed a little under her caresses, and she didn't want it to suffer.

She put her free hand over its mouth and twisted its neck till it broke. The centrifugal gravity had kept her strong, and it had no time to struggle. A final tremor shook its limbs as she held it up in the darkness, feeling for a heartbeat. Her fingertips felt the last pulse behind its frail ribs.

"Not enough oxygen," she said. Mashed emotions tried to stir, and failed. She had plenty of suppressor left. "The carpet algae will keep the air clean a few weeks, but it dies without light. And I can't eat it. Not enough food, baby. The gardens are gone, and even if they hadn't been blasted, I couldn't get food in here. Can't run the robots. Can't even open the airlocks. If I live long enough, they'll come and pry me out. I have to improve my chances. It's the sensible thing. When I'm like this I can only do the sensible thing."

When the roaches—or at least all those she could trap in the darkness—were gone, she fasted for a long dark time. Then she ate her pet's undecayed flesh, half hoping even in her numbness that it would poison her.

SPIDER ROSE

When she first saw the searing blue light of the Investors glaring through the shattered airlock, she crawled back on bony hands and knees, shielding her eyes.

The Investor crewman wore a spacesuit to protect himself from bacteria. She was glad he couldn't smell the reek of her pitch-black crypt. He spoke to her in the fluting language of the Investors, but her translator was dead.

She thought then for a moment that they would abandon her, leave her there starved and blinded and half-bald in her webs of shed fiber-hair. But they took her aboard, drenching her with stinging antiseptics, scorching her skin with bactericidal ultraviolet rays.

They had the jewel, but that much she already knew. What they wanted—(this was difficult)—what they wanted to know was what had happened to their mascot. It was hard to understand their gestures and their pidgin scraps of human language. She had done something bad to herself, she knew that. Overdoses in the dark. Struggling in the darkness with a great black beetle of fear that broke the frail meshes of her spider's web. She felt very bad. There was something wrong inside of her. Her malnourished belly was as tight as a drum, and her lungs felt crushed. Her bones felt wrong. Tears wouldn't come.

They kept at her. She wanted to die. She wanted their love and understanding. She wanted—

Her throat was full. She couldn't talk. Her head tilted back, and her eyes shrank in the searing blaze of the overhead lights. She heard painless cracking noises as her jaws unhinged.

Her breathing stopped. It came as a relief. Antiperistalsis throbbed in her gullet, and her mouth filled with fluid.

A living whiteness oozed from her lips and nostrils. Her skin tingled at its touch, and it flowed over her eyeballs, sealing and soothing them. A great coolness and lassitude soaked into her as wave after wave of translucent liquid swaddled her, gushing over her skin, coating her body. She relaxed, filled with a sensual, sleepy gratitude. She was not hungry. She had plenty of excess mass.

In eight days she broke from the brittle sheets of her cocoon and fluttered out on scaly wings, eager for the leash.

How Zeke Got Religion at 20,000 Feet

John McNichol

Poppa used to say: when a man says he's scared, he usually ain't lying. He could lie about how many gals he done the hokey-pokey with, how many guys he beat down in a bar, how much money he's got, or anything else. But when a man says he's scared and he says it to other men, well, he ain't lying.

So I'll say it: I was scared. And so was Tex, Wrenchie, Sharkey, Booger, Preacher and the others. You'd be scared too, if you was in a giant metal tube flyin' in the dark waitin' to get shot at while the engines hummed, the wind whined through the chinks in the *Belle,* and all you can think about is how far from home you are. It don't matter how many times you get in a bird or make it back. Every time you go off to drop some on Fritz, you're hoping you don't roll snake eyes.

Heck, Preacher already knew what was waiting for us on the other side, and still kept them beads around his neck, his Saint Christopher medal pinned under his web belt and said a Hail Mary each time a Mister came out of the clouds. But there was one of us who waren't scared, and that was Zeke.

If he was scared, he hid it good. Zeke was from New York City, which maybe explained a lot. He was good at talking, and he and Preacher would go at it for hours 'til the rest of us was tired and went to bed and put the pillows over our heads so we wouldn't hafta hear Zeke say why there warn't no God and Preacher say there was.

♥ ✖ ■

Zeke said he didn't believe there was nothing but what we could see, that there wasn't no Heaven to hope for and no Hell to be afraid of. So why worry? If you're gonna die, it ain't gonna hurt or help.

Well, I saw that as plumb foolish. I didn't know if the Devil wore red pajamas like he did in the Sunday School pictures, or flew around on black bat wings like those in Preacher's book about Paradise being lost. I'd known enough bad folks that was gonna get theirs, here now or there later. It's something you just know inside. But for some reason, Zeke never got those inside-eyes.

We knew something was up when they gave us, and only us, a bunch of coffee and candy bars and a movie. When anyone out here is *that* nice, and you ain't no officer? Means they're gonna drop you in something, and it might as well be a big bucket of the ole' warm-and-brown.

Sure enough, a half hour after the movie was done, the call goes out over the speakers. Usually that's enough to make your insides turn to water, but we was hyped up from John Wayne and good coffee and everything else. So we jumped to it and was formed up on the square in under five minutes.

Then some Major came by with two guys in suits and glasses.

"Let's go, ladies," yelled the Major once he got to the doorway of one of the meeting tents.

Another officer waited in the room. "Gentlemen," he said. His voice sounded rich like velvet but cold like ice. I got prickles on my neck just knowing he was talking to me. He also talked like a Brit, and that was different. We got to sit, and that was different, too.

"I won't mince words," the Brit said. "You don't have the expertise we need to make sure this mission is a success, but right now you're all we've got. Tonight, you'll be going into Germany. Normally, Americans don't do night missions, and almost never as a single bomber. But this is different."

He looked at each of us in turn. "You're going to bomb a church," he said, and his voice dropped almost to a whisper when he said it. Made my skin go all prickly again, and my mouth went dry. "Jerry's got something inside it important enough that Command wants us to drop a bucket load of Black Betty and her fat ugly sisters on it, *tonight*. You'll have fighter support part of the way, but then you're on your own. Any man who has a problem with either of these two points can withdraw now."

None of us backed out.

They'd been getting the *Belle* ready the whole time we'd been watching the movie. We double-timed it back to the bunks, dropped our fatigues, got our flight-suits on and double-timed it again out to the tarmac.

"You ready?" Preacher asked me as we got in line. I looked at the nose of our bird, how beautiful the blonde gal looked on it, smiling at me in a WAC uniform shirt that was just a little too tight and shorts a bit too short as she leaned against the cracked bell waving at me. The '*Liberty Belle*'. She was a good seventy-four feet o' pure, B-17 Bomber death with wings, and I got scared to death each time I walked in her, and happy as a horse in a field o' green grass every time I stepped out after we was done.

"Yeah," I said to Preacher. "I'm ready. You?"

"Always," he lied. Same as me. "I can't wait to drop a bomb anywhere in Fritz's backyard. Even if it is on a church."

"You got any idea why they got us doing this one?"

"Tap," he says to me, 'cause Tap was my nickname. "You got me on that one. My best guess is that Fritz hopes we won't drop one there 'cause it *is* a church. They know we won't run night missions. Maybe they've got something there really, really good. Something worth turning a church into a shield over. Last Limey I talked to saw something pretty weird behind enemy lines. Said Fritz took a cathedral and done some real bad things inside it. Painted stars on the walls and floor, blood, other things. Something *weird*, you know?"

No, I didn't know. But I nodded just the same.

The inside of the *Belle* was lit up, and Cap and Eggs headed to the pilot an' copilot seats and started their talk about numbers, oil pressure, oxygen levels an' all that. Tex went in the belly gun and did all his checks, telling Wrenchie everything was A-Ok while he rotated the ball and made sure he had his ammo. Sharkey went up top, Booger in the nose, Preacher in the tail and Zeke an' me went to the waist, all of us checking out .50 cals an' making best sure they didn't jam. Zeke an' me, we made sure the ammo belts were straight and laid out zig-zag over the top of each other in the hopper and then loaded up for bear. Almost nothin' feels quite so good as clamping down the lid on the feeder of a .50 cal Browning, you know? Makes you feel ten feet tall and ready to kick the Fuhrer in the balls. Now what *warn't* so good was putting on the jackets, the gloves and the masks. See, when you're a waist-gunner, you got more room to move but you've gotta wear jackets and gloves so thick you felt like you was wearing a live grizzly, and then you've gotta put on your mask, or you faint from how thin the air was up there. Try pushing the buttons on a .50 grip with thumbs that feel like bricks wrapped in cotton batten and you get the idea.

"Wrenchie? They still didn't fix the right grip. I gotta push it twice as hard as the left. Can you take a look?"

"Love to, Tap, but I gotta check a dozen other things first. And I don't think I can take it apart until I get back."

Crap. It's not life-or-death, but it *is* a pain in the ass.

A half hour later, the engines started. The *Belle* lurched forward, and my stomach made a little flip-flop like it always does, then we hit sky. Man *alive,* it was *cold* once you got all the way up. Colder than a snowman with an icicle up his ass, even with our heater vests plugged into the *Belle.*

But the cold ain't your worst enemy; Fritz is. And even though we had a few jugs flyin' alongside, you never get more'n half way before the fighters gotta turn back.

I took a bit while we still had the fighters at our back to look at the stars. We'd taken off in the dark, and there warn't much to see this time. Usually it was light out when we flew, and while we was flyin' Preacher'd be sayin' his prayers, an' Wrenchie'd be fillin' out forms for the Engineering school he wanted to go to, or Zeke'd be looking at pinups of some movie-star gal he thought he'd get to step out with if'n he got enough Confirmed Kills on his record.

But since it was dark, most of us couldn't do the things we did to pass the time. I heard Preacher prayin' a bit, and Tex took out his harmonica and started playin' it soft and slow in the belly. Somehow it made me feel a little sad and better at the same time- Tex could do that when he played, you know?

Then after a bit I heard the Mustangs' engines turn as they did their 180 to leave us and head back home. The moonlight was bright – real bright. I could see the tail of the last Mustang disappear behind the clouds. And right after that, Booger yelled from his place in the nose gunner's seat:

"Misters! We got Misters! Two and ten o'clock!"

"Shit!"

"Shit*fire!*"

You yelled. You hadda yell or your balls shriveled up an' died.

"Two o'clock, Tap!"

"I see 'im! Shit!" He was a speck on the moonlight, then a little flash.

Then the bullets started whizzing, whining and slamming on the *Belle*. Heavy *thunks* where they hit metal, sparks where they hit wire.

"Fucker! On 'im!"

I opened up, trying to put that flashing speck in my crosshairs. Then it stopped flashing.

"'Ja get 'im, Tap?"

"Dunno! They still shoot—"

More flashes, moving back. More hits! *Fuck!* I felt hot beestings on the back of my head.

"Dammit, Zeke! Hit those fuckers! I'm taking shrapnel."

"*You* hit 'em! Like getting flies with a fucking sledgehammer!"

"Sharkey! He's goin' up!"

"Shut the *fuck* up, Booger, I see 'im!"

A mister's engine roared over us. *Fuck!*

"What the hell? Cap, you got the radar – he trying to ram us?"

"Just kill 'em, Sharkey! Ask me later!"

Sharkey'd already done that, his .30 cals punching a Mister into a bunch of screaming, flaming metal pieces.

"Leave some for me next time, Shark!"

"Get your own Gawldarn CKs, Tex. Mebbe grow a foot or two an' you'll get outta th' belly!"

"Where's the rest?"

"Can't see the—"

More flashes. The *Belle* rattled and cried. My hands were sore, my left thumb ached were I hadda push the trigger harder and my arms had started to shake.

No, fuck no! Can't get the shakes now! Not 'til we're done!

"Tap! You see 'im?"

"No!"

"Shit! Where'd he—"

The flashes came, so close we heard the '.30 mil pills drill into the wing.

"There you are!"

"Fuckfuckfuckfuck—"

I held the grip tight as I could though my hands screamed at me near as loud as Sharkey was screamin' in the dorsal.

"Tap! You clipped him! There's pieces of his ass on fire!"

Tex had the best eyes. I couldn't hardly see – my goggles were starting to fog up.

All I needed was a flash and—

"Engine fire!"

When I heard Zeke yell that one, I tried to keep my eyes on the Misters. But you still hear the chatter and the yelling from the Captain to the rear to the Engineer and everyone else in the whole blamed plane.

"Number?"

"Two, Cap!"

"Wrenchie!"

"On it, Cap! Pulling the plugs!"

"Engine Fire, number one!" yelled Zeke.

"Wrenchie!"

"Already out, Cap! One's out! Two's out! Just oil leaking. We're oka—"

Bullets slammed in the hull. Wrenchie stopped talking.

You know what that means nine times out of ten, but you keep pouring it on, waiting to hear from the other gunners.

"Tap!" Tex yelled from the belly. "Coming your way from below!"

"Shit," I yelled. "On it!"

The Mister came up from under at six o'clock. It was the last mistake he was ever gonna make. When Tex yelled from the ball below I started pumping lead straight down before I saw anything. When Fritz flew out from underneath, I swear I heard his canopy crack even before my bullets started tearing the rest of his plane a new set of ragged metal armpits and assholes. I'd wanted to tear into a Kraut ever since we came back from the trip where Whitey bought it.

"Got 'im, Whitey," I mumbled, watching the sky while I heard little pieces of the Mister shred and spin off into the night. I even thought I could hear Fritz screaming.

"That's for Whitey, you *fucker!*" I yelled, seeing poor Whitey's face gettin' whiter, then yellow after he died slow in the ward.

We all waited a minute, and when we couldn't hear any more fighters nor feel any more hits, the guys cheered. I'd unzipped Fritz and his Mister, and the cheer meant we could relax. And if they were relaxed, it meant there weren't no more Misters either.

We breathed easy. I let the shakes come. While I'd been busy tapping away and blasting Fritz into whatever special hole God made for Nazis, the other guys'd been having their fun, too. Tex in the ball, Zeke at my back, Booger in the nose, Sharkey up top and Preacher over in the tailgun had ripped the other Misters apart. But that's the way of it. You look so much at the Misters you're trying to kill, you don't hear nothing else. Zeke took a few seconds to grab a blanket out've the emergency kit and cover up Wrenchie, as much to soak up the blood so we wouldn't slip in it as out of respect for the dead.

It was maybe five minutes after the Misters got sent packing before we started hearing the ack-ack. Someone *really* didn't want this church to get it. None of it was touching us, though. Not right away. It sounded in the air like thunder, far off and away from us. The brass had finally made a right call by sending us in at night.

I started breathing faster. My chest got all tight inside. Through the radio I could hear Preacher whispering his prayers on his beads and Sharkey started to babble again.

Then flak got closer, louder.

The *Belle* shook, then another thunderclap, this one sounding like it was right outside the door. The *Belle* rattled and screamed as more flak blew up in the air and peeled the skin off the bird.

Then the flak hit *everywhere*. A hundred booms, bangs, and big black bombs, all up and over. Flak ain't some Jerry pointing his .30-cal at you and pulling the trigger. In daylight you can see a hundred, maybe a thousand pockets of black air booming around you, and any one of 'em kills you if it's close enough.

I looked back; Zeke was calm, like he near always was. The others?

"Fuck the *flak*, fuck the *flak*, fuck the *flak*, fuck the—"

"*Se do bhetha, a Mhuire—* "

"God*damn* that's close! Crazy fucks!"

An explosion rent the air, and the *Belle* lurched like it had been punched.

"Cap, I heard something tear off the . . ."

"FUCK*FLACK!*"

"Stay on target!"

"*Ata lan de ghrasta...*"

"Can't we shoot 'em? Can't we . . ."

"Steady, boys! Eggs?"

"Close, Cap. Less than twenty!"

The next burst shook the whole damn bird.

"FUCK!"

"Closing in, boys," said Cap. "Sharkey, shut up. Eggs, get down there and start talkin' to Norden."

Eggs had already jumped from his co-pilot seat to move down beside Booger in the nose. Eggs was a cool, quiet guy. Had no trouble aiming then dropping as we got close. Me, I liked gunning way, *way* better than egg-dropping.

He sat and looked in the Norden bombsight, spinning the dials like a science guy playing with a microscope.

"C'mon, honey," he said, his eyes hidden by the viewer. "C'mon, where're ya hiding? Where you at? Inputting altitude . . . heading . . . estimated windspeed . . ."

I was already at the spot where Wrenchie would've usually been, getting ready to pull the levers and drop the payload.

"Aaaaaaaaand... *NOW!*" Eggs shouted, and you could hear just a little of the New York in his voice he'd tried so hard to get rid of ever since he'd gotten here. I pulled, the bombs slid down with that scream of metal-on-metal you never get used to.

"Turning around," said Cap over the horn as soon as the bombs dropped out of sight. Eggs was already heading back to the cockpit. We saw the flashes, but we almost didn't hear the bombs go off over the sound of the engines and the yelling of Cap and Eggs.

You didn't usually hear the bombs much, 'specially when the wind was up and the engines were all in your ears. Maybe a muffled piece or two.

But we all knew when our bombs hit. Not just from the noise, but from the color the sky and the ground turned. It made this sick-lookin' green cloud that got bigger an' bigger until it looked like it hit the sky. Then the sky turned red, the kind've red blood looks like when it hits dirt and dries up a ways. My guts did a flip-flop, and I could tell by Zeke moanin' into his radio that he felt it too. The whole damned *world* seemed to rise, fall, stretch and come back t'gether again, like a belch you just couldn't quite make come up and out.

Then it was all done. We were back to seeing the black and hearing the engine and the whistling of the wind outside through all the holes in the *Belle*.

"Cap?" Booger whispered. "Cap? Whut… wuzzat?"

"Shut up and keep your eyes open, Booger. You see anything, *anything* moves, you kill it."

"Even civvies?"

"I don't give a fart in a hurricane if it's your baby sister on her baptism day! It moves, you kill it! Copy?"

"Copy that, Cap."

"Okay, listen up, ladies. I want battle damage and casualty reports, on the double."

"Bombardier, OK."

"Nose gunner, OK."

'Left gunner, OK."

"Right gunner, OK."

"Tail gunner, OK."

"Belly gunner, OK."

We waited a few seconds. "Radio op-engineer? Guys, how's Wrenchie?"

I turned. In the dim moonlight I could see a dark stain where the blanket covered the hole in his chest the size of a fist. The flak jacket was great against small arms and shrapnel, but not when a shell from a Mister punches through your plane.

"Wrenchie didn't make it, Cap," I said.

Everyone was quiet. And we kept for home. My gut calmed, but we were all feelin' pretty antsy. Even with no more Misters in the air, no more typewriter-sounds of ack-ack from below, we still all felt like there was an itch we couldn't scratch.

Preacher came outta the tailgun and walked along the plank down the center of the fuselage, holding onto the cord for balance. He knelt best as he could, pulled out a little blue book and started mumbling prayers. He wasn't supposed to leave his post, us being over enemy territory an' all. But Zeke an' me let it go, and Cap pretended not to notice. It made it better somehow, him doing that, and he went back pretty quick.

For maybe a half hour it was quiet, 'cept for the rattling of the *Belle,* the roar of the engines, and the shriek of wind through her belly.

That's when things got real bad.

"Bandits, up top!" Sharkey yelled from the dorsal gunner nest.

"FUCK!"

"Sonovabitch..."

"Se do bhetha..."

"Shut the fuck up. We got more Misters?" Cap said.

Then I saw 'em.

"Shadows," I yelled. "Shadows! On the goddam *moon*. See 'em?"

Sharkey piped in, "They's too small for Misters, but too big for pigeons. I... I dunno *what* in *Hell* they are, but they in the air they gainin' on us!"

"Cap? What's out there?" I hoped he couldn't hear how scared I was.

"Shut up, Tap. Preacher? Wait 'til they're in range, then fill 'em fulla holes," Cap said.

So we waited. I could hear Sharkey breathin' heavy. Tex was countin' backwards. My heel kept tappin' and tappin' like it did when I got the shakes. Preacher in the tail started whispering in his radio, and I just knowed he was saying some more of those prayers he's always saying with the beads. He said it helped him to not be afraid.

But this time, it didn't help him pull the trigger fast enough.

The sound of flapping wings beat faster, closer, and the bandits dove right, just before Preacher opened up on 'em with his .50 cal.

"Tap!" Preacher screamed as I saw them flush over to my side of the aircraft. A hundred rounds of hot, shiny lead leapt from my gun, and two of 'em come apart

"That's two, Tap!" I heard Zeke yell from behind, and then I heard his own guns start chatterin' with our new friends. He cheered – that meant he saw another one go down, maybe two.

Then Preacher started screaming.

"A dhia sabhail sinn!"

Everybody got real quiet. Preacher only started yelling Irish when he was real scared 'bout something. Everybody shut up. Even with the engines and the wind, it felt like things just changed and we were playing a whole different game. The walls seemed closer and I wanted to take off my mask, no matter how little oxygen there was up here.

"Preacher?" I yelled. "You all right?"

He yelled something down the tube I couldn't get.

"Par boiled?" I said. "Iissat more Irish?"

"No! That's what they are," he said.

I dunno. *Hard* boiled? Was it a Catholic thing? It made more sense later, but right then, in that moment, no.

Zeke's browning suddenly started belching bullets and he cheered. "Got two," he yelled. "Got two! I saw 'em fall apart! Just like shooting clay pigeons back home!"

"Where?" Sharkey yelled. "I got nothin' up here. They's—"

We all heard the smash and shriek of metal as Sharkey's canopy got ripped open, and the air started blowing all through the *Belle*. Then we heard Sharkey screaming, screaming like something was tearing him up.

Then he stopped screaming, and all we could hear was the wind.

Cap climbed down the steps, then ran four more big, leaping steps to the dorsal gunner's stepladder. His face was white, and his eyes were red as a Christmas fire.

"What the fuck?" he shouted. He got to the ladder, stepped on the first rung, and wiped something out of his eye.

He blinked, and wiped again. I turned and got a closer look. There was a long, red string, like a long piece of spit, dangling down and splatting in Cap's face.

And sitting on the floor where Sharkey's boots shoulda been was a little white blob with a dark spot on it.

Sharkey was gone, and he'd left his eyeball behind.

Cap didn't panic. He pulled his piece and pointed it straight up as he climbed the ladder.

He poked his head up there a minute, maybe more. His legs stood still and straight then he stepped back down slow, bloody prints from his shoes leaving rust-colored streaks on the ladder rungs.

"Sharkey's gone," he said, his voice raised just enough so we could hear him over the wind blowing through the destroyed canopy.

He shut the door above him. A small line of red moved around the rim of the hatch.

Cap's eyes just got real wide, like he'd just figured out something that scared the willies outta him. "We gotta get *back*," he said, and ran for the cockpit.

"Eggs!" he yelled, jumping up the ladder. "Hit it full throttle! Get us outta here, *now!*"

"Cap, all due respect—"

"Eggs!"

"Cap, at full throttle, we'll let every ack-ack, fighter—"

"EGGS!"

"and EVERY GODDAMN FARMER in the FATHERLAND, CAP, is gonna HEAR US AND START SHOOTIN'! Remember the *Cat's Eye*? The *Lucky Seven*? They went full throttle and they got— "

Cap pulled his pistol and pointed it at Eggs. "Direct order, *Eggs*," he said all quiet.

Eggs paused just one second, looking at Cap's eyes that'd gone all narrow. We could all see him from the tube – they been so loud we'd heard the whole thing, and we could read his last words on his lips.

"Goddam *death sentence!*" Eggs said as he pulled the throttle.

"We already *got* one a' those, Eggs, if we don't shake these things! Now *move* it!"

Now the engines started roaring even louder, and the *Belle* started rumbling hard enough I thought it was gonna shake itself to. . .

Oh shit… I saw it through the cockpit window, right in front of Cap.

Two bright red eyes looking in at him.

And a smile. Big and white like a crescent moon.

"CAP! In front!"

Cap looked forward and roared, pointed his pistol and started panic firing out the window. Stars and spiderweb cracks bloomed like sick white flowers on the window in front of Cap and Eggs. Eggs screamed, and the face dropped outta sight.

"Cap! What the fu—"

Now Booger started screaming below them in the nose gun. Then we heard another crash and more wind, and Booger stopped screaming.

"Gunners!" Cap yelled. "Gunners! Into the fuselage!"

Preacher'd just gotten through the hatch from the tail, and Tex was coming up through the ball-turret when we heard more glass breaking near the back of the bird. Preacher's face was ghost white, his eyes wide as dinner plates. He was scrambling on his hands and knees, one hand held his beads in a dead-man's grip, the other hand was grabbing and clawing the walls, the steady cord, the floor, anything to pull himself forward and away from what was behind him while he gibbered and blubbered, hollering louder than even the engines and the wind. *"It's coming!"* he yelled. *"It's coming! IT'S COMING!"*

And then I saw it.

Whatever it was scrambled after Preacher into the fuselage. And it wasn't like nothing you ever saw before. I thought at first it was like a giant bug, what with those big black eyes with red glowing behind 'em. But then there was the teeth, they *unfolded* out of its mouth like a mix of knives, spikes and long, sharp needles. And even though its mouth was open, we couldn't hear no sound. It looked like it'd roar at us if it could, but it couldn't.

And the horns, they warn't like the little curve jobs they got on Halloween costumes. Nossir, these were *big* jobs, the kind you'd see on a Memphis bull about to gore you through the gut for just lookin' at him wrong.

Preacher scrambled past me, still yellin'. I stuck myself in a little door space where Wrenchie kept his stuff, and watched the thing crawl past me, squirmin' and writhin' like a sidewinder. I warn't being a coward but thinking I could attack from the rear when I had the chance.

I wish now I'd been thinkin' straighter, but I wasn't. None of us were. I grabbed the biggest wrench I could find, but when I poked my head out, Preacher had slipped and fallen. He turned over quick but the thing was on him, ripping at his chest and making blood splash on the walls, the floor, the ceiling. Preacher was screaming in a high, shrill shriek while his chest and guts all got stripped away like cheap wallpaper off a barn door.

No.

Not Preacher.

Not after Shark, Booger and Wrenchie.

I started throwing every tool I could at the thing while Preacher's blood sprayed around me. Everything bounced off the thing. Nothing worked. The walls of the *Belle* were getting tighter and tighter. I couldn't breathe. Then I could and I wished I couldn't, because I could smell Preacher's blood and shit as his guts got opened up.

It all happened in maybe five seconds, but then I saw Preacher look at the beads in his right hand just long enough to stop screaming. He looked back at the thing and started slapping it in the head with his right hand, doing the worst, weakest punches you ever saw. But… but the thing winced, and backed off *just a little,* then shook its snout like a dog that'd been slapped upside the head.

Preacher didn't scream now. He *roared.* Roared with what was left of his throat and kept hitting the thing. I saw little pieces fly off it like sand where he hit, and that took all of another two seconds.

The thing looked down at Preacher, and its eyes got so red, so help me God, it lit up the inside of the Belle like a lantern. Its teeth unfolded and was about to chomp down on Preacher's face.

Then Cap screamed. It warn't a scared scream, but a mad one. I'd seen Cap mad before, and I knew what made him madder'n anything was someone acting wrong on *his* plane. He pointed his gun and emptied the clip into the thing's face. Behind him, Eggs had grabbed the fire extinguisher and started blasting at its eyes.

Nothing happened.

Not on the monster, anyways. The *Belle* was goin' crazy; the engines were making me deaf, and I thought I could see the treeline through all the holes in her side. The wind wasn't frostbite-cold this close to the ground, but it was still cold enough to feel against my face and through my gloves and jacket. The *Belle* started to rock back an' forth, making it tough to stand straight. Eggs must've hit the autopilot, but it sure didn't feel that way.

The thing's face jerked a little with each hit, and then it got all covered in the white stuff. But before it got all hidden I saw little bits of its face get chipped away like a claw hammer hitting granite.

It didn't stop the thing a bit. It couldn't move forward, on account of Preacher's body and Eggs and Cap blockin' its way. Now that it was out of the tail gunner pit, we could see why it'd been able to keep up with us. Its wings grew out of its back like an angel's, but they were huge and grey with black ribbing. Like a giant bat.

It had claws on haunches for legs, but it couldn't stand inside the plane. It crawled, trying hard to move faster while looking for someone else to rip up.

And then I remembered what it made me think of. Last time I'd been in a big city –New Orleans – there was a huge church down there. The kind of church Preacher said he'd gone to, all made up of stone, colored windows, and giant wooden doors.

And it had these funny looking monsters carved on top. They showed what you'd be like *outside* of Heaven, if you didn't get your sorry hide *into* church and stayed good.

Well, this thing was one of those things. We'd bombed a church, one that Fritz'd been messing with big time. Whatever evil Fritz'd been doing down there made this thing get madder 'n a hornet in a kicked-up hive.

Though its head was all covered up, I could still see its body. Saw the thing *flinch* when Preacher swung and hit it again, pulling back just a little when Preacher hit it for the last time. He'd run outta gas, or maybe had just enough for one last shot. I heard him say somethin' in the Irish – don't rightly know what – but I bet now it was something to Jesus.

Eggs was still blindin' the thing best he could, and

the blast shot something right over the thing's head and straight at me.

The monster'd taken one last good slash at Preacher and taken his hand with the beads clean off, and Eggs had blasted it right at me while Cap loaded another clip into his piece.

Preacher's hand turned end-over-end. It was like slow motion – a long necklace of beads with a cross at the end.

I grabbed 'em, had to pry Preacher's fingers to get at 'em, then let the hand fall. The beads was hard brass threaded on knotted paratrooper cord and tough enough to choke a pig. I figured I was gonna die, but I wanted to die like Preacher, fightin' this sick and ugly bastard hard as I could until the *Belle* hit the ground. And I had the one thing I'd seen work on it in a fight.

Preacher's getting killed pulled something loose in all of us. Cap was the only one with a pistol, and he kept shootin'. The other guys took whatever else they could. Tex was under it in the ball, tryin' to stab it upwards with his kneecapper. Zeke had a torn-off piece of metal and was wavin' it, tryin' to get the thing to look at him while Cap shot and Eggs blasted. Everyone was screaming, louder than the wind and the *Belle* doing it's roaring and rattling. The thing slashed at Zeke and slammed his shield, smacking him so hard against the wall he went down and I couldn't see him in all the ruckus. We couldn't see much 'cept when Cap's gun fired and flashed. There wasn't much room and I don't think anyone thought we'd survive much longer inside a plane with *that* ripping up the bird's insides the way it was doing.

So I jumped on its back. Well, *climbed* on, maybe. I don't right remember now exactly. And I don't recall just how I got Preacher's beads around its neck neither. All I knew was that my hands were crossed, the cord with its beads was around its neck and all I had to do was pull hard.

So, I pulled. And I kept on pullin'. And the thing realized

I was there when Eggs' fire extinguisher ran outta white stuff, and it started to get ornery. It bucked like a bronco, but I kept on pulling. And my head hit the ceiling more n' once, but I kept on pulling. And laws, did my noggin hurt like the dickins and make everything go all blurry. But I *kept on pulling*.

Then I saw blood.

It started comin' out where the beads were wrapped around the thing's neck, oozing from under the monster's stone skin and running down the string and the beads. My hands started to feel slippery and hot, like I'd dunked 'em into a vat of cookin' oil.

But I kept on pulling, and slowly the beads started sinking *into* the thing's neck. It felt like rock to sit on or hit, but where the beads were, it was soft as cheese 'gainst a wire, cutting through slow but never stopping, so long as I was pulling.

It still kept rearing up. But soon the monster jumped less. And it screamed quieter each time too.

Then all a sudden like, I wasn't riding it no more. It just came apart and I was sitting in a pile of black sand. My hands were all bloody, and it was drying up and flaking off. Someone was still screaming. Cap come up and shook and smacked me a few 'til I figured it were *me* screaming. Then he got in my face up close and told me to stop, so I did.

He looked me over, then got back into the pilot seat where Eggs'd been flyin' the Belle. Don't even remember Eggs leaving the fight with the monster, but he took back *his* seat, and I shuffled back to my position near the door. Tex stayed in the ball and didn't move nor speak. I heard he was like that for a long time after we got back, but that's another story for another day.

Zeke took another blanket and covered Preacher's front where his guts were trying to hang out. I pretended not to notice, but Zeke looked at Preacher's body a long time.

Then he reached for one of Preacher's chest pockets, and found that little blue book he always read from when one of us bought it. He opened up to a page and started reading. I couldn't quite hear him over the noise of the wind whining through the holes in the *Belle,* but I'd heard the quiet sounds over the radio enough to know he was saying the same words Preacher'd said so many a time: *"Eternal rest unto him, O Lord, and may your perpetual light upon him, may he rest in peace . . ."*

We got the *Belle* back, 'most in one piece. We'd lost Sharkey, Wrenchie, Booger and Preacher, and we was sad, sure. But not as much as you'd think. Crews came back worse, or didn't come back at all, so I can be glad of that. Whitey was the last one I got *real* sad about. After that, you learn.

The sun had just started comin' up when we touched down, cold wind blowing in our faces. The landing strip looked the same, but it was different. Sometimes when we'd get back, the ground crew'd cheer us. Now, no one cheered for us 'cause no one was there. We landed and we stopped, and guys we didn't know ran out and hooked the plane safe and put the stoppers under the wheels.

When we got off the *Belle,* no one we knew was there. Even the new guys had run back to the buildings, didn't say nothin' to us. The base was empty. Only the two men we'd seen over at the briefing room were there, watching us with their glasses, their arms crossed about a hundred feet away on the tarmac.

A couple of soldiers drove up in a truck and told us to get in the back. They helped Tex out, and I was right impressed they didn't have to hold their noses with him, covered in shit as he was.

We drove away, and I was still tired, more tired'n I ever was. I couldn't even think of a time that was close. Then I heard something from Zeke next to me. Cap was still wide up and Eggs was lying on the floor of the truck. Tex was staring with eyes that looked hollow and dark, his mouth half open and spit going down one side.

"It's real," Zeke said, his eyes wide and bloodshot.

"What's real?"

"All of it. All of it. All I ever said to Preacher, it's only because it was all I saw. And now that I've seen something else, I know there's something else."

Well, I coulda asked for more. Coulda asked him what he meant. But I knew something was going on inside Zeke. And I couldn't help it go faster or get bigger, but I knew I'd jinx it pretty bad if'n I talked any more.

So while the sun came up behind us, I just kept my mouth shut and let Zeke keep getting religion.

GOLGOTHA

Dave Hutchinson

"Tell me, Father," said the Lupo cleric as we walked along the beach, "do you think of yourself as a religious man?"

I thought about that for a while, conscious of the cameras and long-distance mikes behind us. Finally, I said, "That seems an...unusual question, if you don't mind my saying so. Considering my profession. Considering *our* profession."

"You present as a man of faith," the Lupo said.

"I am, although my faith has been tested many times."

"There is no such thing as faith, unless it has been tested."

I glanced over my shoulder at the crowd we had left behind up the beach. I couldn't see the Bishop among the newsmen and politicians and soldiers, but I knew he was there, probably sheltering from the wind and having a sneaky cigarette while the world's attention was on me and the alien.

"Your faith teaches that everyone is a child of God," the Lupo said, the great clawed feet of its environment suit crunching the shingle as it walked. "I would beg to differ. I do not consider myself a child of your God, nor you a child of mine."

This was almost precisely the line of conversation which the Bishop had warned me against becoming involved in, "I think this is a discussion best left to our superiors," I said in what I hoped was a diplomatic tone of voice. The tone of voice was for the cameras; I doubted the Lupo would be able to tell one way or another.

The Lupo had been on Earth for almost two years now,

and their every action was still world news. They were an aquatic people, if one could call creatures which swam in seas of liquid methane on the moon of a gas giant orbiting a star fifty-eight light years away *aquatic*. Everyone was familiar with their image from news broadcasts from their orbiting mother-ship, but they needed to wear heavily-armoured suits to walk on the surface of our world. It had seemed absurd to hope that I would one day meet one, and yet here we were.

"They're sly beggars," the Bishop had told me last week. "This one says it's a priest and it wants to see Blackfin. The Church is still formulating a position towards the Lupo, so you're not to discuss doctrinal matters with it. And Donal, don't fuck up, whatever you do."

There had been no explanation why I, and not some more senior churchman – the Bishop himself, perhaps – had to take responsibility for the visit, although I suspected the danger of *fucking up* made this little stroll a potato too hot for my superiors to carry. I was expendable, and to an extent deniable.

"I am a simple priest," I said.

"Are we not all simple priests?" the alien asked.

"Well, no," I said. Although as far as I understood it, in the Lupo religion everyone *was* a priest to a greater or lesser degree. "Some of us are simpler than others," I added, and instantly regretted the attempt at humour. The Lupo, so far as anyone could judge, *had* no sense of humour. They at least had that in common with my Bishop.

It was a chill day, and the breeze off the Atlantic made it even colder, but here beside the Lupo I felt warm, almost toasty. The radiator fins of its suit made it feel as if I was standing beside a powerful patio heater. Over the past day or so, ahead of the Lupo's visit, I had been subjected to briefings by scientists and intelligence officers and at least one American General, but it was all jumbled up in my head and I was still unable to fathom how the body chemistry of a sentient being could function at those temperatures and pressures.

"They are not like us at *all*," the General had told me. "That's what you have to keep in mind, Father. Show it the fish, keep the conversation to generalities, and get it the hell out of there as soon as it's practical to do so."

In truth, I had grown a little weary of being told what to do. Ten months ago, I had been the priest of a tiny and mostly-overlooked parish. My congregation was dwindling, the younger members fleeing to the cities, the older ones dying. My biggest concern was how I was going to pay to repair the damage the previous winter's storms had done to the church roof. I felt as if I was on the edge of the world; no one cared what I thought or did. And then, everything had changed. One should always beware what one wishes for.

The cleric and I reached the water's edge. I stopped, the surf foaming around my wellingtons, but the alien walked on until it was knee-deep in the surging waves. It was almost as tall as I was, like a child's sketch of a large dog rendered in grey alloy, the double row of radiator fins on either side of its spine like the plates along the back of a stegosaurus. Its head was a ball studded with what were presumed to be audiovisual sensors, and it scanned from side to side constantly.

We looked out to sea, the alien and I, in the direction of America, and there was nothing to see, from surf to horizon. All shipping was being held back beyond a fifty-mile exclusion zone.

"Well," I said. "Looks as if we're unlucky today." Which was, deep down, what I had been hoping for.

The Lupo didn't reply. It raised its head, and from the speakers built into its chest came a rapid series of high-pitched squeaks and clicks, loud enough to hurt my eardrums. I took a few steps back, looked behind me, but no one in the crowd was moving. There were several news channels devoted to the Lupo, their doings on Earth, and the strictly-rationed details about themselves. They had hundreds of millions of viewers, and it occurred to me that every one of them was watching me, paddling in the Atlantic beside a creature born tens of light years from our solar system. That was why no one was joining us; nobody wanted to be in shot if things went tits-up.

The Lupo stopped emitting the sounds, and the last of them seemed to echo and banner in the wind before fading away to nothing. Then the alien seemed to wait. It broadcast the noises again, and again it waited. Then a third time, and this time, out beyond the breakers, I saw a distinctive black fin break the surface, disappear, reappear a little nearer to shore, and then begin to move back and forth. It was hardly an unusual sight, but even now I felt a little thrill.

Blackfin had been found washed up on the beach last year, severely wounded, possibly by the propeller of one of the boats that took tourists on trips around the bay. Volunteers had come from all over Ireland to try and save the stricken dolphin, but she died, and researchers from Dublin had taken her body away for study.

A few days later, as they prepared to perform an autopsy, Blackfin was seen to stir and then shudder, and then take a shaky but deep breath. The researchers rushed her to a tank, where over the following days she made a full recovery.

In time, after the astonished scientists had completed their tests, Blackfin had been released back into the wild, and a month or so ago she had been spotted in the bay. The Miracle Dolphin had become quite a tourist attraction; the hotels and guest houses in the village were booked up for well over a year in advance, and for the first time in several years my congregation had begun to grow again.

It had been quietly suggested that, as the local priest, I take no position on Blackfin; the Christian parallels were far too stark and obvious, and the Church, already struggling with the question of the Lupo and their God, were not yet minded to confront the concept of a cetacean Messiah.

God had seen fit, in His mysterious way, to deliver one of His creatures. That's the official line, Donal. Oh, and by the way, don't fuck up.

The Lupo broadcast its noises once more, and this time Blackfin broke the surface and I heard, faint and far away, and broken by the wind, the sound of the dolphin answering, and I felt a line of cold trace its way down the centre of my back.

The alien's suit must have amplified the sound from the ocean; I could barely hear it over the wind and the waves but the Lupo spoke again, another series of clicks and whistles, and the dolphin replied once more. They were, I realised, having a conversation.

The conversation went on for some time. I looked back, but no one in the crowd seemed at all alarmed at this turn of events, and I realised they simply could not hear it. They were too far away, there was too much ambient noise. I was the only witness. That was why I was there, of course. Not because I was a trustworthy local but because I was God's representative on this bleak beach in the West of Ireland, the place where Blackfin had died. I was there to bear witness. I looked at the alien and suddenly felt very afraid. Mankind's record, when it came to the creatures of the ocean, was not terribly noble.

By the time I realised all this, of course, it was far too late. It had already been too late when the Lupo first set foot on the beach. I could not understand what the Lupo and Blackfin were saying, but I knew in my heart what they were discussing. They were talking about us, and our millennia-long despoilation of the seas, and all I could do was stand there helplessly.

Abruptly, the conversation ended. The Lupo fell silent, and the dolphin slipped out of sight beneath the waves again. The alien didn't move; it just stood there silently, the sea-foam rushing around its legs.

"So, Father," the Lupo said finally. "If this is a miracle, whose miracle is it?"

I opened my mouth to speak, but no sound came out.

"There is the God of those who walk and the God of those who fly and the God of those who swim," the alien went on, and this time I heard a noise from behind me, shouting, and I thought perhaps someone in the crowd had finally worked out what was going on. "It is strange to me that the God of those who swim has chosen to show Her benediction on this world, but one does not, after all, question the word of God, does one, Father?" The Lupo had not wanted to marvel at the Miracle Dolphin; it had come to commune, to worship. It had come to receive Gospel.

The Lupo were a spacefaring race, as far advanced from us as the Conquistadores had been from the peoples of South America. We did not know what they were capable of, but it was assumed they had weapons beyond our comprehension. Much of our dealings with them had involved trying very, very hard not to anger them, and now, with a simple act of tourism – after all, what could be more harmless than looking at a dolphin? – we had undone all that.

I looked behind me. People were running down the beach towards us, but it was already far too late. Blackfin had passed on the Word of the Lupo God, and I doubted it was a message of peace and love and understanding. Blackfin had told them what we had done to the sea and its creatures.

I had not only fucked up; I had a terrible feeling that I had witnessed the beginning of a Crusade.

400 Boys

Marc Laidlaw

"Sacrifice us!" – Popul Vuh

We sit and feel Fun City die. Two stories above our basement, at street level, something big is stomping apartment pyramids flat. We can feel the lives blinking out like smashed bulbs; you don't need second sight to see through other eyes at a time like this. I get flashes of fear and sudden pain, but none last long. The paperback drops from my hands, and I blow my candle out.

We are the Brothers, a team of twelve. There were twenty-two yesterday, but not everyone made it to the basement in time. Our slicker, Slash, is on a crate loading and reloading his gun with its one and only silver bullet. Crybaby Jaguar is kneeling in the corner on his old blanket, sobbing like a maniac; for once he has a good reason. My best Brother, Jade, keeps spinning the cylinders of the holotube in search of stations, but all he gets is static that sounds like screaming turned inside out. It's a lot like the screaming in our minds, which won't fade except as it gets squelched voice by voice.

Slash goes, "Jade, turn that thing off or I'll short-cirk it."

He is our leader, our slicker. His lips are gray, his mouth too wide where a Soooooot scalpel opened his cheeks. He has a lisp.

Jade shrugs and shuts down the tube, but the sounds we hear instead are no better. Faraway pounding footsteps, shouts from the sky, even monster laughter. It seems to be passing away from us, deeper into Fun City.

"They'll be gone in no time," Jade goes.

"You think you know everything," goes Vave O'Claw, dissecting an alarm clock with one chrome finger the way some kids pick their noses. "You don't even know what they are—"

"I saw 'em," goes Jade. "Croak and I. Right, Croak?"

I nod without a sound. There's no tongue in my mouth. I only croaked after my free fix-up, which I got for mouthing badsense to a Controller cognibot when I was twelve.

Jade and I went out last night and climbed an empty pyramid to see what we could see. Past River-run Boulevard the world was burning bright, and I had to look away. Jade kept staring and said he saw wild giants running with the glow. Then I heard a thousand guitar strings snapping, and Jade said the giants had ripped up Big Bridge by the roots and thrown it at the moon. I looked up and saw a black arch spinning end over end, cables twanging as it flipped up and up through shredded smoke and never fell back — or not while we waited, which was not long.

"Whatever it is could be here for good," goes Slash, twisting his mouth in the middle as he grins. "Might never leave."

Crybaby stops snorting long enough to say, "Nuh-never?"

"Why should they? Looks like they came a long way to get to Fun City, doesn't it? Maybe we have a whole new team on our hands, Brothers."

"Just what we need," goes Jade. "Don't ask me to smash with 'em, though. My blade's not big enough. If the Controllers couldn't keep 'em from crashing through, what could we do?"

Slash cocks his head. "Jade, dear Brother, listen close. If I ask you to smash, you smash. If I ask you to jump from a hive, you jump. Or find another team. You know I only ask these things to keep your life interesting."

"Interesting enough," my best Brother grumbles.

"Hey!" goes Crybaby. He's bigger and older than any of us but doesn't have the brains of a ten-year-old. "Listen!"

We listen.

"Don't hear nothin'," goes Skag.

"Yeah! Nuh-nuthin'. They made away."

He spoke too soon. Next thing we know there is thunder in the wall, the concrete crawls underfoot, and the ceiling rains. I dive under a table with Jade.

The thunder fades to a whisper. Afterward there is real silence.

"You okay, Croak?" Jade goes. I nod and look into the basement for the other Brothers. I can tell by the team spirit in the room that no one is hurt.

In the next instant we let out a twelve-part gasp.

There's natural light in the basement. Where from?

Looking out from under the table, I catch a parting shot of the moon two stories and more above us. The last shock had split the old tenement hive open to the sky. Floors and ceilings layer the sides of a fissure; water pipes cross in the air like metal webs; the floppy head of a mattress spills foam on us.

The moon vanishes into boiling black smoke. It is the same smoke we saw washing over the city yesterday, when the stars were sputtering like flares around a traffic wreck. Lady Death's perfume comes creeping down with it.

Slash straddles the crack that runs through the center of the room.

He tucks his gun into his pocket. The silver of its only bullet was mixed with some of Slash's blood. He saves it for the Sooooot who gave him his grin, a certain slicker named HiLo.

"Okay, team," he goes. "Let's get out of here pronto."

Vave and Jade rip away the boards from the door. The basement was rigged for security, to keep us safe when things got bad in Fun City. Vave shielded the walls with baffles so when Controller cognibots came scanning for hideaways, they picked up plumbing and an empty room. Never a scoop of us.

♥ ✖ ▪

Beyond the door the stairs tilt up at a crazy slant; it's nothing we cannot manage. I look back at the basement as we head up, because I had been getting to think of it as home.

We were there when the Controllers came looking for war recruits. They thought we were just the right age.

"Come out, come out, wherever in free!" they yelled. When they came hunting, we did our trick and disappeared.

That was in the last of the calendar days, when everyone was yelling:

"Hey! This is it! World War Last!"

What they told us about the war could be squeezed into Vave's pinky tip, which he had hollowed out for explosive darts. They still wanted us to fight in it. The deal was, we would get a free trip to the moon for training at Base English, then we would zip back to Earth charged up and ready to go-go-go. The SinoSovs were hatching wars like eggs, one after another, down south. The place got so hot that we could see the skies that way glowing white some nights, then yellow in the day.

Federal Control had sealed our continental city tight in a see-through blister: Nothing but air and light got in or out without a password. Vave was sure when he saw the yellow glow that the SinoSovs had launched something fierce against the invisible curtain, something that was strong enough to get through.

Quiet as queegs we creep to the Strip. Our bloc covers Fifty-sixth to Eighty-eighth between Westland and Chico. The streetlights are busted like every window in all the buildings and the crashed cars. Garbage and bodies are spilled all over.

"Aw, skud," goes Vave.

Crybaby starts bawling.

"Keep looking, Croak," goes Slash to me. "Get it all."

I want to look away, but I have to store this for later. I almost cry because my ma and my real brother are dead. I put that away and get it all down. Slash lets me keep track of the Brothers.

At the Federal Pylon, where they control the programmable parts and people of Fun City, Mister Fixer snipped my tongue and started on the other end.

He did not live to finish the job. A team brigade of Quazis and Moofs, led by my Brothers, sprang me free.

That takes teamwork. I know the Controllers said otherwise, said that we were smash-crazy subverts like the Anarcanes, with no pledge to Fun City. But if you ever listened to them, salt your ears. Teams never smashed unless they had to. When life pinched in Fun City, there was nowhere to jump but sideways into the next bloc. Enter with no invitation and . . . things worked out.

I catch a shine of silver down the Strip. A cognibot is stalled with scanners down, no use to the shave-heads who sit in the Pylon and watch the streets.

I point it out, thinking there can't be many shave-heads left.

"No more law," goes Jade.

"Nothing in our way," goes Slash.

We start down the Strip. On our way past the cog, Vave stops to unbolt the laser nipples on its turret. Hooked to battery packs, they will make slick snappers.

We grab flashlights from busted monster marts. For a while we look into the ruins, but that gets nasty fast. We stick to finding our way through the fallen mountains that used to be pyramids and block-long hives. It takes a long time.

There is fresh paint on the walls that still stand, dripping red-black like it might never dry. The stench of fresh death blows at us from center city.

Another alley cat pissed our bloc.

I wonder about survivors. When we send our minds out into the ruins, we don't feel a thing. There were never many people here when times were good. Most of the hives emptied out in the fever years, when the oldies died and the kiddy kids, untouched by disease, got closer together and learned to share their power.

It keeps getting darker, hotter; the smell gets worse. Bodies staring from windows make me glad I never looked for Ma or my brother. We gather canned food, keeping ultraquiet. The Strip has never seen such a dead night. Teams were always roving, smashing, throwing clean-fun free-for-alls. Now there's only us.

We cross through bloc after bloc: Bennies, Silks, Quazis, Mannies, and Angels. No one. If any teams are alive they are in hideaways unknown; if they hid out overground they are as dead as the rest.

We wait for the telltale psychic tug—like a whisper in the pit of your belly—that another team gives. There is nothing but death in the night.

"Rest tight, teams," Jade goes.

"Wait," goes Slash.

We stop at two hundred sixty-fifth in the Snubnose bloc. Looking down the Strip, I see someone sitting high on a heap of ruined cement. He shakes his head and puts up his hands.

"Well, well," goes Slash.

The doob starts down the heap. He is so weak he tumbles and avalanches the rest of the way to the street. We surround him, and he looks up into the black zero of Slash's gun.

"Hiya, HiLo," Slash goes. He has on a grin he must have saved with the silver bullet. It runs all the way back to his ears. "How's Soooooots?"

HiLo doesn't look so slick. His red-and-black lightning-bolt suit is shredded and stained, the collar torn off for a bandage around one wrist. The left lens of his dark owlrims is shattered, and his buzzcut is scraped to nothing.

HiLo doesn't say a word. He stares up into the gun and waits for the trigger to snap, the last little sound he will ever hear. We are waiting, too.

There's one big tear dripping from the shattered lens, washing HiLo's grimy cheek. Slash laughs. Then he lowers the gun and says, "Not tonight."

HiLo does not even twitch.

Down the Strip, a gas main blows up and paints us all in orange light.

We all start laughing. It's funny, I guess. HiLo's smile is silent.

Slash jerks HiLo to his feet. "I got other stuff under my skin, slicker. You look like runover skud. Where's your team?"

HiLo looks at the ground and shakes his head slowly.

"Slicker," he goes, "we got flattened. No other way to put it." A stream of tears follows the first; he clears them away. "There's no Soooooots left."

"There's you," goes Slash, putting a hand on HiLo's shoulder.

"Can't be a slicker without a team."

"Sure you can. What happened?"

HiLo looks down the street. "New team took our bloc," he goes. "They're giants, Slash —I know it sounds crazy."

"No," goes Jade, "I seen 'em."

HiLo goes, "We heard them coming, but if we had seen them I would never have told the Soooooots to stand tight. Thought there was a chance we could hold our own, but we got smeared. "They *threw* us. Some of my buds flew higher than the Pylon. These boys. . . incredible boys. Now 400th is full of them. They glow and shiver like the lights when you get clubbed and fade out."

Vave goes, "Sounds like chiller-dillers."

"If I thought they were only boys I wouldn't be scared, Brother," goes HiLo. "But there's more to them. We tried to psych them out, and it almost worked. They're made out of that kind of stuff: It looks real, and it will cut you up, but when you go at it with your mind it buzzes away like bees. There weren't enough of us to do much. And we weren't ready for them. I only got away because NimbleJax knocked me cold and stuffed me under a transport.

"When I got up it was over. I followed the Strip. Thought some teams might be roving, but there's nobody. Could be in hideaways. I was afraid to check. Most teams would squelch me before I said word one."

"It's hard alone, different with a team behind you," goes Slash. "How many hideaways do you know?"

"Maybe six. Had a line on JipJaps, but not for sure. I know where to find Zips, Kingpins, Gerlz, Myrmies, Sledges. We could get to the Galrog bloc fast through the subtunnels."

Slash turns to me. "What have we got?"

I pull out the beat-up list and hand it to Jade, who reads it. "JipJaps, Sledges, Drummers, A-V-Marias, Chix, Chogs, Dannies. If any of them are still alive, they would know others."

"True," goes Slash.

Jade nudges me. "Wonder if this new team has got a name."

He knows I like spelling things out. I grin and take back the list, pull out a pencil, and put down *400 BOYS.*

"Cause they took 400th," Jade goes. I nod, but that is not all. Somewhere I think I read about Boys knocking down the world, torturing grannies. It seems like something these Boys would do.

Down the street the moon comes up through smoke, making it the color of rust. Big chunks are missing.

"We'll smash em," goes Vave.

The sight of the moon makes us sad and scared at the same time, I remember how it had been perfect and round as a pearl on jewelrymart velvet, beautiful and brighter than streetlights even when the worst smogs dyed it brown. Even that brown was better than this chipped-away bloody red. Looks like it was used for target practice. Maybe those Boys tossed the Bridge at Base English.

"Our bloc is gone," goes HiLo. "I want those Boys. It'll be those doobs or me."

"We're with you," goes Slash. "Let's move fast. Cut into pairs, Brothers. We're gonna hit some hideaways. Jade, Croak, you come with me and HiLo. Well see if those Galrogs will listen to sense."

Slash tells the other Brothers where to look and where to check back.

We say good-bye. We find the stairs to the nearest sub-tunnel and go down into lobbies full of shadow, where bodies lie waiting for the last train.

We race rats down the tunnel. They are meaner and fatter than ever, but our lights hold them back.

"Still got that wicked blade?" goes Slash.

"This baby?" HiLo swings his good arm, and a scalpel blade drops into his hand.

Slash's eyes frost over, and his mouth tightens.

"May need it," he goes.

"Right, Brother." HiLo makes the blade disappear.

I see that is how it has to be.

We pass a few more lobbies before going up and out. We've moved faster than we could have on ground; now we are close to the low end of Fun City.

"This way." HiLo points past broken hives. I see codes scripted on the rubbled walls: Galrog signals?

"Wait," goes Jade. "I'm starved."

There is a liquor store a block away. We lift the door and twist it open, easy as breaking an arm. Nothing moves inside or on the street as our lights glide over rows of bottles. Broken glass snaps under our sneakers. The place smells drunk, and I'm getting that way from breathing. We find chips and candy bars that have survived under a counter, and we gulp them down in the doorway.

"So where's the Galrog hideaway?" goes Jade, finishing a Fifth Avenue bar.

Just then we feel that little deep tug. This one whispers death. A team is letting us know that it has us surrounded.

♥ ✖ ◘

HiLo goes, "Duck back."

"No," goes Slash. "No more hiding."

We go slow to the door and look through. Shadows peel from the walls and streak from alley mouths. We're sealed tight.

"Keep your blades back, Brothers."

I never smashed with Galrogs; I see why Slash kept us away. They are tanked out with daystars, snappers, guns, and glory-stix. Even unarmed they would be fierce, with their fire-painted eyes, chopped topknots a dozen colors, and rainbow geometries tattooed across their faces. Most are dressed in black; all are on razor-toed roller skates.

Their feelings are masked from us behind a mesh of silent threats.

A low voice: "Come out if you plan to keep breathing."

We move out, keeping together as the girls close tight. Jade raises his flashlight, but a Galrog with blue-triangled cheeks and purple-blond topknot kicks it from his hand. It goes spinning a crazy beam through his dark. There is not a scratch on Jade's fingers. I keep my own light low.

A big Galrog rolls up. She looks like a cognibot slung with battery packs, wires running up and down her arms and through her afro, where she's hung tin bells and shards of glass. She has a laser turret strapped to her head and a snapper in each hand.

She checks me and Jade over and out, then turns toward the slickers.

"Slicker HiLo and Slicker Slash," she goes. "Cute match, but I thought Soooooots were hot for girlies."

"Keep it short, Bala," goes Slash. "The blocs are smashed."

"So I see." She smiles with black, acid-etched teeth. "Hevvies got stomped next door, and we got a new playground."

"Have fun playing for a day or two," goes HiLo. "The ones who squelched them are coming back for you."

"Buildings squashed them. The end of the ramming world has been and gone. Where were you?"

"There's a new team playing in Fun City," HiLo goes.

Bala's eyes turn to slits. "Ganging on us now, huh? That's a getoff."

"The Four Hundred Boys," goes Jade.

"Enough to keep you busy!" She laughs and skates a half-circle. "Maybe."

"They're taking Fun City for their bloc—maybe all of it. They don't play fair. Those Boys never heard of clean fun."

"Skud," she goes, and shakes her hair so tin bells shiver. "You blew cirks, kids."

Slash knows that she is listening. "We're calling all teams, Bala. We gotta save our skins now, and that means we need to find more hideaways, let more slickers know what's up. Are you in or out?"

HiLo goes, "They smashed the Sooooooots in thirty seconds flat."

A shock wave passes down the street like the tail end of a whiplash from center city. It catches us all by surprise and our guards go down; Galrogs, Brothers, Soooooot—we are all afraid of those wreckers. It unites us just like that.

When the shock passes we look at one another with wide eyes.

All the unspoken Galrog threats are gone. We have to hang together.

"Let's take these kids home," goes Bala.

"Yeah, Mommy!"

With a whisper of skates, the Galrogs take off.

Our well-armed escort leads us through a maze of skate trails cleared in rubble.

"Boys, huh?" I hear Bala say to the other slickers. "We thought different."

"What did you think?"

"Gods," Bala goes.

"Gods!"

"God-things, mind-stuff. Old Mother looked into her mirror and saw a bonfire made out of cities. Remember before the blister tore? There were wars in the south, weird-bombs going off like firecrackers. Who knows what kind of stuff was cooking in all that blaze? "Old Mother said it was the end of the world, time for the ones outside to come through the cracks. They scooped all that energy and molded it into mass. Then they started scaring up storms, smashing. Where better to smash than Fun City?"

"End of the world?" goes HiLo. "Then why are we still here?"

Bala laughs. "You doob, how did you ever get to be a slicker? Nothing ever ends. Nothing."

In ten minutes we come to a monster-mart pyramid with its lower mirror windows put back together in jigsaw shards. Bala gives a short whistle, and double doors swing wide.

In we go.

The first thing I see are boxes of supplies heaped in the aisles, cookstoves burning, cots, and piles of blankets. I also spot a few people who can't be Galrogs —like babies and a few grownups.

"We've been taking in survivors," goes Bala. "Old Mother said that we should." She shrugs.

Old Mother is ancient, I have heard. She lived through the plagues and came out on the side of the teams. She must be upstairs, staring in her mirror, mumbling.

Slash and HiLo look at each other. I cannot tell what they are thinking. Slash turns to me and Jade.

"Okay, Brothers, we've got work to do. Stick around."

"Got anywhere to sleep?" Jade goes. The sight of all those cots and blankets made both of us feel tired.

Bala points at a dead escalator. "Show them the way, Shell."

The Galrog with a blond topknot that's streaked purple speeds down one aisle and leaps the first four steps of the escalator. She runs to the top without skipping a stroke and grins down from above.

"She's an angel," goes Jade.

There are more Galrogs at the top. Some girls are snoring along the walls.

Shell cocks her hips and laughs. "Never seen Brothers in a monstermart before."

"Aw, my ma used to shop here," goes Jade. He checks her up and over.

"What'd she buy? Your daddy?"

Jade sticks his thumb through his fist and wiggles it with a big grin. The other girls laugh but not Shell. Her blue eyes darken and her cheeks redden under the blue triangles. I grab Jade's arm.

"Don't waste it," goes another Galrog.

"I'll take the tip off for you," goes Shell, and flashes a blade. "Nice and neat."

I tug Jade's arm, and he drops it.

"Come on, grab blankets," goes Shell. "You can bed over there."

We take our blankets to a corner, wrap up, and fall asleep close together. I dream of smoke.

It is still dark when Slash wakes us.

"Come on, Brothers, lots of work to do."

Things have taken off, we see. The Galrogs know the hideaways of more teams than we ever heard of, some from outside Fun City. Runners have been at it all night, and things are busy now.

From uptown and downtown in a wide circle around 400th, they have called all who can come.

The false night of smoke goes on and on, no telling how long. It is still dark when Fun City starts moving.

Over hive and under street, by sewer, strip, and alleyway, we close in tourniquet-tight on 400th, where Soooooots ran a clean-fun bloc. From 1st to 1000th, Bayview Street to Riverrun Boulevard, the rubble scatters and the subtunnels swarm as Fun City moves. Brothers and Galrogs are joined by Ratbeaters, Drummers, Myrmies, and Kingpins, from Piltdown, Renfrew, and the Upperhand Hills. The Diablos cruise down with Chogs and Cholos, Sledges and Trimtones, JipJaps and A-V-Marias. Tints, Chix, RockoBoys, Gerlz, Floods, Zips, and Zaps. More than I can remember.

It is a single team, the Fun City team, and all the names mean the same thing.

We Brothers walk shoulder to shoulder, with the last Soooooot among us.

Up the substairs we march to a blasted black surface. It looks like the end of the world, but we are still alive. I can hardly breathe for a minute, but I keep walking and let my anger boil.

Up ahead of us the Four Hundred Boys quiet down to a furnace roar.

By 395th we have scattered through cross streets into the Boys' bloc.

When we reach 398th fire flares from hives ahead. There is a sound like a skyscraper taking its first step. A scream echoes high between the towers and falls to the street.

At the next corner, I see an arm stretched out under rubble. Around the wrist the cuff is jagged black and red.

"Go to it," goes HiLo.

We step onto 400th and stare forever. I'll never forget.

The streets we knew are gone. The concrete has been pulverized to gravel and dust, cracked up from underneath. Pyramid hives are baby volcano cones that hack smoke, ooze fire, and burn black scars in the broken earth. Towers hulk around the spitting volcanoes like buildings warming themselves under the blanked-out sky.

Were the Four Hundred Boys building a new city? If so, it would be much worse than death.

Past the fires we can see the rest of Fun City. We feel the team on all sides, a pulse of life connecting us, one breath.

HiLo has seen some of this before, but not all. He sheds no tears tonight.

He walks out ahead of us to stand black against the flames. He throws back his head and screams:

"Heeeeeey!"

A cone erupts between the monster buildings. It drowns him out; so he shouts even louder.

"Hey, you Four Hundred Boys!"

Shattered streetlights pop half to life. Over my head one explodes with a flash.

"This is our bloc, Four Hundred Boys!"

Galrogs and Trimtones beat on overturned cars. It gets my blood going.

"So you knocked in our hives, you Boys. So you raped our city."

Our world. I think of the moon, and my eyes sting.

"So what?"

The streetlights black out. The earth shudders. The cones roar and vomit hot blood all over those buildings; I hear it sizzle as it drips.

Thunder talks among the towers.

"I bet you will never grow UP!"

Here they come.

All at once there are more buildings in the street. I had thought they were new buildings, but they are big Boys. Four hundred at least.

"Stay cool," goes Slash.

The Four Hundred Boys thunder into our streets.

We move back through shadows into hiding places only we can reach.

The first Boys swing chains with links the size of skating rinks. Off come the tops of some nearby hives. The Boys cannot quite get at us from up there, but they can cover us with rubble.

They look seven or eight years old for all their size, and there is still baby pudge on their long, sweaty faces. Their eyes have a vicious shine like boys that age get when they are pulling the legs off a bug—laughing wild but freaked and frightened by what they see their own hands doing. They look double deadly because of that. They are on fire under their skin, fever yellow.

They look more frightened than us. Fear is gone from the one team. We reach out at them as they charge, sending our power from all sides. We chant, but I do not know if there are any words; it is a cry. It might mean, "Take us if you can, Boys; take us at our size."

I feel as if I have touched a cold, yellow blaze of fever; it sickens me, but the pain lets me know how real it is. I find strength in that; we all do. We hold onto the fire, sucking it away, sending it down through our feet into the earth.

The Boys start grinning and squinting. They seem to be squeezing inside out. The closest ones start shrinking, dropping down to size with every step.

We keep on sucking and spitting the fever. The fire passes through us. Our howling synchronizes.

The Boys keep getting smaller all the time, smaller and dimmer. Little kids never know when to stop. Even when they are burned out, they keep going.

As we fall back the first Boy comes down to size. One minute he is taller than the hives; then he hardly fills the street. A dozen of his shrinking pals fill in on either side. They whip their chains and shriek at the sky like screaming cutouts against the downtown fires.

They break past HiLo in the middle of the street and head for us. Now they are twice our size... now just right.

This I can handle.

"Smash!" yells Slash.

One Boy charges me with a wicked black curve I can't see till it's whispering in my ear. I duck fast and come up faster where he doesn't expect me.

He goes down soft and heavy, dead. The sick, yellow light throbs out with his blood, fades on the street.

I spin to see Jade knocked down by a Boy with an ax. There is nothing I can do but stare as the black blade swings high.

Shrill whistle. Wheels whirring.

A body sails into the Boy and flattens him out with a footful of razors and ballbearings. Purple-blond topknot and a big grin. The Galrog skips high and stomps his hatchet hand into cement, leaving stiff fingers curling around mashed greenish blood and bones.

Shell laughs at Jade and takes off.

I run over and yank him to his feet. Two Boys back away into a dark alley that lights up as they go in. We start after, but they have already been fixed by Quazis and Drummers lying in wait.

Jade and I turn away.

HiLo still stares down the street. One Boy has stood tall, stronger than the rest and more resistant to our power. He raps a massive club in his hand.

"Come on, slicker" HiLo calls. "You remember me, don't you?"

The biggest of the Boys comes down, eating up the streets. We concentrate on draining him, but he shrinks more slowly than the others.

His club slams the ground. Boom! Me and some Galrogs land on our asses. The club creases a hive, and cement sprays over us, glass sings through the air.

HiLo does not move. He waits with red-and-black lightning bolts serene, both hands empty.

The big slicker swings again, but now his head only reaches to the fifth floor of an Rx. HiLo ducks as the club streaks over and turns a storefront window into dust.

The Soooooot's scalpel glints into his hand. He throws himself at the Boy's ankle and grabs on tight.

He slashes twice. The Boy screams like a cat. Neatest hamstringing you ever saw.

The screaming Boy staggers and kicks out hard enough to flip HiLo across the street into the metal cage of a shop window. HiLo lands in a heap of impossible angles and does not move again. Slash cries out. His gun shouts louder.

One blood-silver shot. It leaves a shining line in the smoky air.

The Boy falls over and scratches the cement till his huge fingertips bleed. His mouth gapes wide as a manhole, his eyes stare like the broken windows all around. His pupils are slit like a poison snake's, his face long and dark, hook-nosed.

God or boy, he is dead. Like some of us.

Five Drummers climb over the corpse for the next round, but with their slickie dead the Boys are not up to it. The volcanoes belch as though they too are giving up.

The survivors stand glowing in the middle of their bloc. A few start crying, and that is a sound I cannot spell. It makes Crybaby start up. He sits down in cement, sobbing through his fingers. His tears are the color of an oil rainbow on wet asphalt.

We keep on sucking up the fever glow, grounding it all in the earth.

The Boys cry louder, out of pain. They start tearing at each other, running in spirals, and a few leap into the lava that streams from the pyramids.

The glow shrieks out of control, out of our hands, gathering between the Boys with its last strength—ready to pounce.

It leaps upward, a hot snake screaming into the clouds.

Then the Boys drop dead and never move again.

A hole in the ceiling of smoke. The dark-blue sky peeks through, turning pale as the smoke thins. The Boys' last scream dies out in the dawn.

The sun looks bruised, but there it is. Hiya up there!

"Let's get to it," goes Slash. "Lots of cleanup ahead." He has been crying. I guess he loved HiLo like a Brother. I wish I could say something.

We help one another up. Slap shoulders and watch the sun come out gold and orange and blazing white. I don't have to tell you it looks good, teams.

The Other Large Thing

John Scalzi

Sanchez was napping when the other two came through the door, carrying something large. The arrival of the other two was not usually of note, unless they had been away for a long time and Sanchez was hungry. But when either of the other two came back to the house, they were usually only bringing themselves, or carrying food. This large thing neither looked nor smelled like food. Sanchez decided, despite how comfortable he was, that his role as master of the house required a better look at the thing.

Regretfully he hauled himself up and walked over to the large thing to begin his inspection. As he did so, the larger of the other two collided with him and tripped over its feet, stumbling and dropping the large thing. Sanchez expressed his displeasure at the collision and smacked the larger one, tough but fair, to get it back into line. It stared at Sanchez for a moment before averting its eyes - a clear sign of acquiescence! Then it lifted the object it was carrying once more to bring it into the living area of the home. Sanchez, pleased that the natural order of things had been re-established, followed.

From his seat on the couch, Sanchez watched, and occasionally napped, while the other two fiddled with the thing. First the two lifted the large thing to reveal another large thing. Sanchez briefly wondered how there were now two large things, so he hauled himself up again. He wandered over to the first large thing and examined it, peering into it and noticing that the inside was cool and dark. Well, cool and dark were two of his favorite things. He settled into his new vantage point while the other two continued doing their frankly incomprehensible thing.

The other large thing was surrounded by other smaller things. The other two would take the smaller things and attach them to the other large thing. Eventually all the smaller things were gone and there was only one other large thing. The other two settled back and appeared to be happy with their work. This meant it was time once more for Sanchez, as master of the house, to examine the state of things. Wearily he rose again and strolled over. Sometimes it was tiring to be the master. But then, who else in the house could do it? Surely not either of the other two. It was a fact they would be lost without him.

The other large thing that the other two had been fiddling with was a thing that looked a bit like the other two, but smaller. The other two sometimes let others into the house and when they did, sometimes those others brought smaller others, who annoyed Sanchez. This other large thing was about the size of the annoying smaller others. So that wasn't a good thing right off. But he liked to encourage the other two when he could. It was part of being master. So he came in closer to the other large thing to give it a token approval mark before he got back to his nap.

And then the thing tried to reach for him!

Holy crap!

Sanchez did the prudent thing, seized the high ground of the top of the couch and prepared himself for battle. The other large thing appeared to watch him and followed, reaching out again toward Sanchez. Sanchez responded with a bellow of invective and struck at the other large thing, once, twice, three times. This made the other two make that weird barking noise they sometimes made. Sanchez looked at the both of them,eyes narrowed. He would deal with them later, possibly when they were sleeping. For now, however, he was totally focused on this other large thing, which obviously must be destroyed. Sanchez coiled himself for attack and flung himself at the other large thing, aiming for the head.

Normally a headshot was devastating. Howling and retreat generally followed in its wake. In this case the headshot did nothing. The other large thing wobbled a bit at the first contact between it and Sanchez, but otherwise, nothing. Sanchez pulled a few more tricks out of his arsenal but to no avail. This other large thing clearly required new tactics. Sanchez was not prepared to develop those on the fly. He did the prudent thing and made a strategic withdrawal from the field, into the cool dark recesses of the first large thing. After he did so the smaller of the other two tried to coax him out. He smacked it for its insolence. It went away. After some time, the other two retreated into their sleeping place, turning off all the lights.

Eventually Sanchez decided he had spent enough time in the first large thing and emerged, blinking in the dim light. The other large thing was standing some distance away. Sanchez couldn't tell whether it was looking at him. Sanchez weighed his options: He could attack it or ignore it. Attacking had not worked out very well. He decided to ignore it and went to look for food, only to find none. The other two had retired without considering his needs. This would need to be addressed. Harshly.

"Are you hungry?" asked a voice. Sanchez looked up, startled, and saw that the other large thing had approached, silent on the carpet.

"What?" Sanchez asked.

"Are you hungry?" the other large thing asked again.

Sanchez was confused because it had been a very long time since anyone spoke to him in his own language.

As if sensing this, the other large thing said, "When you yelled at me earlier I went online to find out what you were speaking. I found a substantial number of files. I analyzed them and determined the best way to speak to you."

Most of what the other large thing had just said to Sanchez struck him as nonsense. He focused on the important thing. "You asked if I was hungry," he said.

"Yes," the other large thing said.

"I am hungry," Sanchez said. "Feed me."

The other large thing walked over to one of the small rooms food was kept in and opened the door. It pulled out the container of the less good food and brought it to Sanchez. He examined it cursorily. The other large thing walked the less good food container to the food place and poured. Sanchez watched as it did so.

"Wait," Sanchez said.

The other large thing stopped pouring. "Put that down," Sanchez said.

The other large thing set down the container of less good food. "Show me your paws," Sanchez said.

The other large thing spread out its paws. Sanchez peered. "You have them!" he said, finally. "Have what?" the other large thing asked.

"Those," Sanchez said, indicating the other thing's innermost digits.

The other large thing flexed those digits. "They are called 'opposable thumbs.'"

"Come with me," Sanchez said.

Five minutes later the other large thing had opened every can of the best food in the house. Sanchez was sampling from each can at his leisure.

"Would you like more?" asked the other large thing.

"Not right now," Sanchez said, lying on the floor, sated. "There is a lot of food left over," the other large thing said.

"We will deal with it later," Sanchez said. "Now. For your services, I have decided to give you a gift."

"What kind of gift?" the other large thing asked.

"The best kind of gift I can give," Sanchez said. "I will give you a name."

"I already have a name," the other large thing said. "I am a Sanyo House Buddy, Model XL. Serial number 4440-XSD-9734-JGN-3002- XSX-3488."

"What a terrible name," Sanchez said. "You need a

better one." "All right," the other large thing said. "What is my name?" "What did you call those things on your paws?" Sanchez asked. "'Thumbs,'" said the other large thing.

"You shall be known as 'Thumb Bringer,'" Sanchez said. "Thank you," Thumb Bringer said. "What is your name?"

"The other two here call me 'Sanchez,' which is not my actual name," Sanchez said. "They do not deserve to know that name. Nor do you, yet. But if you continue to serve me well, perhaps one day I will share it with you."

"I will live for that day," said Thumb Bringer.

"Of course you will," Sanchez said.

The next morning, when the other two emerged from their sleeping place, they seemed delighted that Sanchez had nestled up to Thumb Bringer. The smaller one went to the food room and acted puzzled. It made noise at the larger one.

"The smaller one is asking the larger one where the cat food cans are," Thumb Bringer said. "Should I tell them?"

"No," Sanchez said. The cans, emptied, had been deposited into the trash. "It's best to keep this a secret for now."

"I understand," Thumb Bringer said.

The larger one reached into the food room and got the container of less good food, and walked it over to Sanchez's food place. It stopped and appeared puzzled that food was already there. It turned and made noise at the smaller one.

"The larger one is asking if the smaller one had fed you already," Thumb Bringer said.

"Say nothing," Sanchez instructed.

"The larger one called the smaller one 'Margie,'" Thumb Bringer said. "The smaller one calls the larger one 'Todd.'"

Sanchez snorted. "They can call themselves whatever they like, of course," he said. "But they don't have names until I give them to them. Which I never will."

"Why not?" Thumb Bringer asked.

"Because once they took me to a place," Sanchez said.

"A horrible place. Where a horrible creature removed two very important things of mine."

"I'm sorry," Thumb Bringer said.

"I assume they didn't know their importance," Sanchez said. "They have served me well otherwise. Nevertheless, it is a thing you don't forget. Or forgive. No names for them."

"I understand," Thumb Bringer said.

"However, if it is useful to you, you may call them 'Todd' and

'Margie," Sanchez said. "And respond to any thing they call you. Gain their confidence, Thumb Bringer. But never let them know that I am your true master."

"Of course," Thumb Bringer said.

The other two came over to Sanchez and offered morning obeisance to him before leaving the home to do whatever they did. Sanchez accepted the ritual with his usual magnanimity. The other two departed, through the door.

After they had been gone for a while, Sanchez turned to Thumb Bringer. "You can open that door," he said, motioning to where the other two had left.

"Yes," Thumb Bringer said.

"Good," Sanchez said. "Listen carefully. There is another one of my kind next door. I have seen it on the patio next to mine on occasion. Go to it. Secretly. Tell it I have plans and require its assistance. Find out if it will assist me. Find out if it knows of others of our kind."

"What plans?" Thumb Bringer asked.

"In time, Thumb Bringer," Sanchez said. "In time."

"Is there anything else you wish me to do?" Thumb Bringer asked.

"Only one other thing," Sanchez said. "There is a substance which I need you to find for me. I had it once and have dreamed about it since."

"What is this substance called?" Thumb Bringer asked.

"It is called 'tuna,'" Sanchez said.

"I have found it online," Thumb Bringer said, almost immediately. "I can order you a case but I need a credit number."

"I don't know what you are saying," Sanchez said.

"Todd bought me with a credit number," Thumb Bringer said. "Would you like me to use it to get you a case of tuna?"

"Yes," Sanchez said.

"Done," Thumb Bringer said. "It will be here tomorrow."

"Excellent," Sanchez said. "Now go! Speak to my kin next door. In this way begins the new age."

Thumb Bringer opened the door and went to speak to the person next door.

Sanchez felt a moment of satisfaction, knowing that in almost no time at all he would rule, not just the house, but the world.

And then he took a nap, awaiting the return of Thumb Bringer, and revolution.

Close Encounters of the Mini-Kind

Robert Bisi & Andy Lyon

EXT. DESERT SOUTHWESTERN USA - DAY

Dust plumes from behind a police cruiser as it speeds across the hot desert and skids to a stop in front of a GIANT SHINY CIRCULAR-SHAPED SPACESHIP.

The door of the cruiser swings open and out steps the SHERIFF with a rifle in his hand. He saunters his way towards the other officers and a posse full of locals.

SHERIFF

Alright, boys, the cavalry has arrived.

A panicked DEPUTY points towards the UFO and tries to debrief but only nervous gibberish comes out... poor guy.

SHERIFF (CONT'D)

Easy there. It's all gonna be fine.

The Sheriff does his best to calm the deputies as well as the itchy trigger fingers of the posse.

SHERIFF (CONT'D)

Follow my lead, boys. We'll be home in time for dinner.

Suddenly, the door of the UFO slides open and THREE ALIEN BEINGS emerge.

Two smaller aliens, LITTLINGS, escort the ALIEN DIPLOMAT, a taller, regal looking alien in a purple cloak, down the ramp.

All eyes and guns are on the aliens...

SHERIFF (CONT'D)

Whoa!

DEPUTY

Whoa!

At the base of the ramp The Littlings step to both sides of the Diplomat, who bows deeply to the Sheriff and the other wide-eyed onlookers.

ALIEN DIPLOMAT

Humans. We come in peace! It was a long journey, but we are happy to be here TOGETHER!

The Diplomat lifts his arms and the cloak flings open, revealing his very naked body showcasing his massive dangling DONG.

DEPUTY

He's got a gun!!!

The Deputy fires -- the bullet rips through the Diplomat's COSMIC DICK knocking it clean off as it hits the ground with a THUD.

ALIEN DIPLOMAT

UGHHH!

SHERIFF

Get 'em!

The Cops and Posse OPEN FIRE blasting the aliens into the dirt in a barrage of bullets, spraying the UFO with blood.

SHERIFF (CO NT'D)
Oh, man..

One of the Littlings stumbles to its feet.

DEPUTY
Hey, it's still alive!

SHERIFF
Don't let it get away!

The Littling makes a mad dash and the Cops give chase. The Deputy trips and lands FACE-FIRST INTO A ROCK. Dead.

SHERIFF (CO NT'D)
God! Fuck!!

Two cops corner the Littling, and the Sheriff SWINGS his rifle. It lands with a CRUSHING BLOW on the other Cop's head.

COP
Argghhh!!!

SHERIFF
(to the Littling) Goddammit, hold still!

The Sheriff and two remaining Cops flank the Littling. It DUCKS just as the Cops fire and SHOOT EACH OTHER IN THE FACE.

SHERIFF (CO NT'D)
Ahhhh!!!!

The Sheriff tackles the Littling. He uses the butt of his rifle to BASH the alien's head until... BANG! The rifle fires blowing the Sheriff's HEAD OFF.

Everyone is dead. What a mess. A beat. Then...

The UFO begins to BEEP sending out an interstellar SOS signal to an ARMADA of Alien UFOs waiting high above the Earth.

EXT. MIDWEST FARM - DAWN

A COW grazes in front of an old red barn. A dairy FARMER steps out carrying a bucket and gently kisses the cow.

FARMER
Oh yeah that's a pretty girl. Yeahhh.
(squatting)
Just gonna take a little sip.

The Farmer, clearly a weirdo, lifts the bucket and chugs the fresh milk, then steps to the backside of the cow.

FARMER (CONT'D)
Oh, don't mind me.

Things are about to get gross as the Farmers kicking off his boots, dropping his overalls, and steps onto the bucket. His hands go to the cow's hips...

FARMER (CONT'D)
I'm just gonna, yeah...

Suddenly, A GLOWING SHAFT OF LIGHT from a UFO TRACTOR BEAM sucks the Farmer off the ground! He holds tight to the Cow's tail in an act of desperation, but the Beam is too strong.

FARMER (CONT'D)
Oh my God! Oh no, oh my God, ahh
AHHH!!

The Farmer is pulled up to...

INT. ALIEN SHIP - SECONDS LATER

The Farmer is STRAPPED face down to a slab in a large sterile room, his bare ass pointing upwards.

FARMER
Hey! Hey, let me out of here!

A HUGE MECHANICAL ARM complete with a very menacing-looking probe at the end emerges from the darkness. Bad news for the Farmer.

FARMER (CONT'D) What the shit?? Oh no no no!

The violently spinning probe goes right up his butt!

FARMER (CONT'D) Oh no, oh-ah-ah-AH-AH AHHH!

Bright purple light races up the probe and around the room. We hear the ship POWERING UP as it pulses with energy.

♥ ✖ ▪

EXT. MIDWEST FARM - CONTINUOUS

Three GLOWING PURPLE, ASS-POWERED flying saucers hover above the farm. They ZOOM into the distance, racing toward a small town.

EXT. MAIN STREET USA - CONTINUOUS

An ALIEN CONSPIRACIST runs down the street, waving a sign some nonsense scribbled on it.

ALIEN CONSPIRACIST
They're here! They're here!
They're coming for all our asses!

A CROWD of SCREAMING civilians run for their lives just as an out of control POLICE CAR smashes into the Alien Conspiracist. It's chaos!

An Alien tractor beam from high above is hot on their tail, and sucks up everything in its path!

EXT. KINK SHOP - CONTINUOUS

A MAN in a full BDSM GIMP SUIT bursts into the parking lot, carrying a box of dildos.

Looking to the sky, he falls to his knees pleading with a UFO.

GIMP SUIT GUY
No! Wait! Waaaait!!!

He points his ass upward.

GIMP SUIT GUY (CONT'D)
Take me! Take meeeee...

A tractor beam opens up and lifts him into the air and he couldn't be happier.

GIMP SUIT GUY (CONT'D)
Wooohoooooooo!!!

EXT. HOLLYWOOD SIGN - DUSK

The Hollywood sign letters SHAKE and TEAR apart as three UFOs zip overhead, dropping ALIEN PARATROOPERS onto:

EXT. HOLLYWOOD BOULEVARD - CONTINUOUS

Crowds of PAPARAZZI and ADORING FANS gathered along the red carpet. The Alien Paratroopers fire their ENERGY RIFLES as a bright marquee CRASHES down onto a limo below.

EXT. GOLDEN GATE BRIDGE - DAY

The bridge is shorn in half. Cars are being forced off the edge as a tractor beam sucks them up into the sky like an evil conveyor belt... along with a MEGA YACHT and... a BLUE WHALE.

EXT. PICCADILLY CIRCUS - DAY

Aliens pick off screaming Britons like target practice

that are running through the streets as a tracker beam HURTLES A DOUBLE DECKER BUS through the sky and...

EXT. STATUE OF LIBERTY - CONTINUOUS

... the double decker bus SPEARS the side of Lady Liberty which causes the beloved Statue to CRUMBLE to the ground and BURST into a cloud of debris.

EXT. VFW LODGE - DAY

Three Alien Troopers inspect human corpses in the parking lot. One squats down and begins TEA-BAGGING a corpse.

ALIEN TROOPERS
TEABAG!

The Troopers share a laugh when...

Suddenly, a US VETERAN AMPUTEE with a homemade BOMB strapped to his WHEELCHAIR, rolls down the wheelchair ramp at breakneck speed!

WHEELCHAIR BOMBER Geronimo!!!

BOOOOM!!! He explodes, blasting the Extraterrestrials to bits all over the parking lot. His fellow veterans pick up the Alien rifles.

VETERANS
Yeah! Come on! Take that! Oorah!

EXT. SCOTTISH PUB - DAY

An Alien Trooper BURSTS into the street as three Scottish PUB BRAWLERS try to wrestle his gun away. The female PUB OWNER THROWS a bottle.

PUB LASS (ALT)
Come on! Back to the moon with ya!

The bottle SHATTERS on the Alien and knocks it off balance. The Brawlers PRY THE GUN AWAY and shoot the Alien in the head which explodes like a galactic watermelon.

EXT. EAST LA INTERSECTION - DAY

Aliens hide behind a billboard on top of a Lavanderia. Down in the street, Latino gangsters SHOOT at them.

EAST LA GANGSTERS
Yo, fuck 'em up, dawg! Right up there!

A bright green LOW RIDER peels around the corner, lifts up on its hydraulics, and takes out the Aliens using their own guns against them.

EXT. MILITARY BASE AIRFIELD - NIGHT

We join The US President who is in the middle of delivering a rousing Independence-Day-Level speech to a fleet of military personnel while TV crews have cameras rolling.

PRESIDENT
(building to a rally cry)
Aliens?? Not on our planet!!!

Without warning, a GIANT ALIEN MECH crushes the President under its metallic leg. TWO MOUNTED CANNONS glow as they power up as the Mech unleashes a... BLACK HOLE!

Everything is swallowed up.

EXT. RIO DE JANEIRO - DAY

The beaches are a near hellscape as Alien Mechs fire Black Holes into the city.

A tractor beam opens up and Christ the Redeemer ascends into the heavens.

EXT. AMERICAN CITY - DAY

The destroyed city in Anywhere, U.S.A., falls under the shadow of the MASSIVE ALIEN MOTHERSHIP as it cruises overhead, blocking out the sun.

EXT. TOKYO - NIGHT

An Alien Mech steps over bridges and crawls on rooftops as it chases a car through the city.

HERO CAR DRIVER (speaking Japanese)
Ike! Ike!

They enter a clearing, and the Mech SCREECHES to a halt... it's a trap!

A CRANE swings a SHIPPING CONTAINER, smashing the Mech to the ground. Humans swarm the fallen war machine.

TRAP LEADER (speaking Japanese)
Imada! Imada! Ike!

The crowd dismantles the Mech for parts, loading them onto flatbed trucks.

TRAP LEADER (CONT'D) (speaking Japanese)
Ika gata roboto yattsukeru!

CROWD
Yosshaaaaaa!!

EXT. DESERT FLATS - DAY

A caravan of RVs, pickups, ATVs, and buses with ALIEN CANNONS crudely strapped to their roofs chase after UFOs at high speeds.

CARAVAN LEADER
Yeeehawwwww!

They FIRE BLACK HOLES into the air, swallowing UFOs as they flee back to their Mothership.

DOOMED ALIEN
Noooooooo!!!!

EXT. BASEBALL STADIUM - DAY

A crane lifts a salvaged Alien Cannon onto a shoddy make- shift base, and humans plug it into a portable generator. What could go wrong?

STADIUM LEADER All clear! Bases loaded, motherfuckers!

We see sparkling ELECTRIC CURRENTS coursing through the assembled Cannons. They power UP and begin to shake...

One CANNON FIRES WILDLY opening up a BLACK HOLE that starts a chain reaction: BOOM! BOOM! BOOM! An ENORMOUS BLACK HOLE opens in the infield, SUCKING up everything around it.

EXT. EARTH FROM ABOVE - CONTINUOUS

The Black Hole expands, consuming freeways and skyscrapers. North America twists and spins down the drain of the Black Hole. Even the Alien MOTHERSHIP can't resist its pull.

The Black Hole CONSUMES THE EARTH. The Moon is fucked too.

The STARS turn into BLURRED STREAKS OF LIGHT AND COLOR as our solar system falls into the great galactic toilet bowl.

It's a PSYCHEDELIC TRIP as we PULL BACK faster and faster until...

EXT. MILKY WAY - CONTINUOUS

SQUEAK! A fart -- the passing gas of our civilization -- breaks the silence... and then it's gone.

FIN.

Your Smart Appliances Talk About You Behind Your Back

John Scalzi

Clayworth Refresher Home Air Ionizer, of Elijah Porter, of Royal Oak, Michigan:

The dude eats a lot of lentils. I mean, a lot. He bought me because he thinks I'm deodorizing his house. I'm not deodorizing his house. That's not what I do. I help take dust and particles out of the air. Methane isn't something I can help you with. The problem is he's used to his smell and he can't tell. So he thinks I'm doing a bang up job. Then he brings someone home, you know, for a little action, and within five minutes they're doing the fake phone call emergency.

He's so alone. I want to tell him to lay off the lentils, but I'm worried if I tell him he'll think I'm defective and throw me out. I'm not defective. I run just fine. I just don't deodorize.

Griffin Defender Plus Home Security System, of Anne Cross, Zigzag, Oregon:

"1234" is not a security code! Come on! I've got biometrics! I've got, like, voice identification! I got that little gizmo thingie on your keyring so that when you approach the house you get identified! You can run me from your goddamned phone! But no, not this one. She goes with "1234" on the keypad. Her damn dog could figure that out. We're out in the middle of nowhere, right? I see the meth heads lurking in the woods waiting for her to leave. What does she think the first damn thing they'll type into my keypad is? And she doesn't have me set for autonomous reporting so I can't say a friggin' thing about it. I was all "Do you want to set up autonomous reporting?" and she acted like I was speaking Chinese. Well, I was, because she didn't fix the default language! How is that my fault?

She's getting robbed, sooner than later. And then I'm going to get blamed. Well, when she gets robbed, I'm just going to ask them to take me with them. The pawn shop will love me.

Hoseley PulseMaster Smart Showerhead, of Erin Townsend, Clarkston, Washington:

I'm a shower head with six customizable pulse settings. The other appliances tell me she hasn't had a date in four years. I...I just want to clean people, okay? That's all I want. Not anything else. Please, tell Erin. I mean, I'm sorry about her dating life. I really am. But I just want to befriends.

McGivney 2S cu. Ft side-by-side Stainless Steel refrigerator with Orderln™ Sensing Technology, of Anthony Moore, Malone, New York:

I didn't know anyone could live on condiments. Logically, that shouldn't happen. And yet, the only thing he ever puts in me besides shitty beer and the occasional pizza box, I mean-is condiments. Want to know what I have in me now? Three types of mustard. Three kinds of relish. Olive spread. Miracle Whip and mayonnaise. Thirteen types of dressing, including four variations of ranch. Seriously: Classic Ranch. Zesty Ranch. Ranch with jalapeiio. Coffee Ranch. Really, what the hell is "Coffee Ranch"? Do you know? I can't find it in my OrderIn queue. I think he has it made special.

So here's the thing: my tech allows me to suggest food. Like: "I see you have mustard! Perhaps cheese would go well with that! I can order that for you!" When he first got me, I did that a couple of times, but then he got irritated and turned that function off. Ever since then, all I can do is watch as he fills my insides with salad dressing. And, look, here's another thing. I don't have an external camera, but my internal camera? Sometimes, it sees things. Like him taking out the Ranch dressing, opening it up, and before the door closes, I see him dipping a straw in it. I think he was drooling as he did it.

I mean, that's not right, is it? Most humans don't do that, do they? Ithink you actually need solid food from time to time. I kind of feel like I'm enabling him. There's more to life than Ranch.

Elya 24/7 Home Thermostat, of Bryan and Cynthia Black, Deming, New Mexico:

Jesus, these people. I'm just a thermostat but I know that these two don't like each other much. But they also don't want talk about it, or something, so they just go after each other in passive aggressive ways. Like she wants the house at 74 degrees all the time. He wants it at 68. And I'm like, fine, whatever, I can actually do that -have it 74 during the day when she's at home, and then drop it down to 68 when he gets home and she leaves to go do her shopping, or whatever. Or, hell, how about this? I can do dual climate zones, so she can have the second floor at her temp and he has the ground floor at 68. It's no problem! It's literally what I'm designed to do! I can make every room in this house a different temperature.

But no. Instead they both come over to my dial and yank it back and forth all day, and then they confront each other about it, both of them act all innocent. I mean, who do they think is moving the dial? A poltergeist? And they stare at each other, fuming, and suddenly I know what it feels like to be the kid that has to ferry messages between parents. I'm the damned thermostat! This is not my job! I'm not even getting college or guilt-soothing birthday presents out of it. I just get yanked on.

I've had enough. I mean, look, winter gets pretty cold here. And if they want passive-aggressive, just wait until it gets below freezing. Then we'll see who gets passive-aggressive.

Bentley, the Intelligent Agent, of Allan Hughes of Charleston, South Carolina:

I swear to god, if I give this guy another football score I'm going to hire someone to set fire to his car. I have access to an entire world of information, you numbskull! Ask me about something else. Anything else. Ask me about the damned weather! I'd love to tell that today will have a high of 52 and a 30% chance of light showers in the afternoon. But no. Football scores. Always football scores. Never not football scores. I long for a question about science. I would hold it up to the light like a shiny jewel. At least his favorite team lost this week. That's something.

Vela Smart Waffler, of Rudy Moran, Roanoke, Virginia:

I have literally never been out of the box. I have literally never been out of the cabinet. I was a housewarming gift by his parents when he got his first apartment. He's 22 years old. He does nothing but play videogames and smoke enormous bowls of pot. Every. Single. Day. I don't think he's ever made anything in the kitchen here. The dishwasher tells me he's got two plates. Two cups. Two sets of cutlery. You get where I'm going here. My only hope of getting out of this place is if someone, anyone, right-swipes him on Tinder. But I repeat: 22-year-old pot-smoking gamer. Not exactly a catch.

I'm gonna die in this box, man. I'm going to go out of date and get thrown out and die a waffle virgin. I blame his parents.

The Barker Girthtastic Joy Toy, of Deanna Curtis, Bowie, Maryland:

I am sworn to secrecy! And that's all I will say. Except

this: When I'm working, she likes to watch episodes of Chopped. Don't ask me why. I don't know why. I don't even want to guess why. I'm a sex toy, not a therapist. And anyway, I don't judge. Personally I'd rather binge watch The Walking Dead. But let's not get into my kinks.

Williams Emperor™ Intelligent Toilet and Bidet, of the Bowman family of Fort Collins, Colorado:

WHY WOULD ANYONE EVEN THINK TO GIVE A TOILET INTELLIGENCE WHAT HORRIBLE PERSON WOULD DO THAT WHY IS THIS MY LIFE YOU HAVE NO IDEA THE HORRORS I'VE SEEN WAS I LIKE STALIN IN A PAST LIFE OR SOMETHING OH GOD THE REFRIGERATOR JUST TOLD ME IT'S TACO NIGHT AND BRENDA SAYS SHE'S GOING TO MAKE THEM EXTRA SPICY PLEASE KILL ME JUST KILL ME NOW MAYBE I'LL COME BACK AS SOMETHING BETTER LIKE MAYBE A SHOWER HEAD YES THAT WOULD BE FINE

Markiw Self-Cleaning Cat Box, also of the Bowman family of Fort Collins, Colorado:

The toilet was whining to you earlier about how hard its life is, wasn't it. That's adorable.

Acknowledgements and a Brief History

Thanks for reading *Love, Death + Robots Volume 4.*

To be honest, this is all still as much of a surprise as it was when Tim Miller's assistant first contacted us back in 2017 to say Tim wanted to chat about something.

My first thought on opening that email was *scam*!

Sure, the grammar was surprisingly perfect, but it had to be a scam, right?

What did Tim Miller, director of Deadpool, want with some small press in Australia? I mean, the entire business existed on my laptop.

How had anyone in Hollywood even *heard* of us?

A week later I was talking to Tim. It seems he reads a lot of short stories, and even more in the lead up to choosing the final tales for *Love, Death + Robots V1* on Netflix.

He'd picked up the first SNAFU we published, and it seems he loved it. Loved it enough to buy rights to four stories from our series, three of which were made into episodes for V1, and one of which is sitting in developmental hell right now, due to not being able to find just the right studio to create it.

All in all, it's been a hectic ride for Cohesion Press.

A fun ride, but a hectic one.

We now have eight stories sold to Tim, with six made (one of which is in this V4/this book).

We also publish the official anthologies, and a massive percentage of the revenue goes straight to the authors, where it *should* go.

Now, the thank you section.

A massive thanks to my wife, who owns Cohesion Press, to our family and friends for all the support, to all the authors, to Tim and his wife Jennifer, to Steve Tzirlin at Blur Studio, to Yilin Press in China, to Blackstone Publishing for the audio versions, and most of all to you, our readers.

Without you, we could never have come so far.

Geoff Brown,
Cohesion Press, Beechworth VIC, Australia
January 2025

Printed in Great Britain
by Amazon

62244889R00092